LYNNE RUSSELL

Heels
of
Fortune

The
PJ Santini
Series

PRAISE FOR *HELL ON HEELS* AND LYNNE RUSSELL

"CNN's Lynne Russell is back, in an explosion of page-turning talent. Get your best bottle of wine, your favorite couch, and prepare for one wild night with *HELL ON HEELS*. It's a helluva read!"   —Craig Nelson, bestselling author of *Rocket Men* and *The First Heroes*

"P.J. Santini, the heroine of *HELL ON HEELS*, is the love child of Janet Evanovich and Elmore Leonard. Lynne Russell's spunky private eye had me at P.J.'s peeing into a one-pound coffee can during stakeouts. It is just so Jeff Bridges' burnt-out country singer in *Crazy Heart*, before the love of a good woman took all the piss out of him."   -Rita Zekas, *Toronto Star*

"Step aside Jack Reacher, PJ Santini is the new bad ass on the scene, actually a very fine ass to be precise. In *HELL ON HEELS* her debut caper she busts chops and cops, while tricked out in her push up bras, thigh highs and skimpy bikini panties...when she's not going commando. Nobody's playmate but easily a future Miss November, we can't wait for her next titillating adventure."

   —Jeff Cohen, Exec Editor/ Publisher *Playboy* Special Editions, Playboy Enterprises

"*HELL ON HEELS* should come with a WARNING label! Lynne Russell's masterful depiction of female Investigator P.J. Santini can literally raise your pulse rate to dangerous levels. The brilliantly crafted insights a reader gets into the thought processes of the clever, gutsy, tough-talking, yet sexually vulnerable Santini, is alone worth the price of admission."

        -Ted Kavanau, Founder of CNN HEADLINE NEWS

"Hilarious! P.J. Santini's hard-boiled detective banter is as sharp and sexy as her stilettos. A humour-mixed-with-murder mystery romp featuring a roster of brash street-smart characters, in this fast-paced riff on hard-boiled detective fiction. "

-Rhonda Rovan, Beauty Editor,
Best Health/Readers Digest Canada

"P.J. Santini is actually Lynne Russell late at night with wine, lights out, imagination gone wild. Both of them are Columbo without the cigar and appendage. Oh the joy of thinking you've been invited to ride shotgun and look for her weapons stash."

-*Moby-In-The-Morning*, Moby Enterprises

"A news anchor with the personality of a professional wrestler."

-*The New York Times*

"Talk about a Renaissance woman, Lynne Russell does it all!"

-Warner Bros. Television

About the Author

Lynne Russell anchored *CNN* and *CNN Headline News* from 1983 to 2001, the first woman to solo anchor a network nightly newscast. Her long-standing dedication to the people's right to know was recognized in *The New York Times*, which called her a "just-the-facts stalwart of CNN Headline News". The *Times* also called her a news anchor with the personality of a professional wrestler, which she took as a compliment. In the *Washington Journalism Review*, she won a spot as "Best in the Business". A private investigator and former deputy sheriff, Lynne now writes romantic crime novels. She an her husband split their time between Washington, D.C. and Italy.

About PJ Santini

PJ SANTINI LIVES IN an uncharted corner of Lynne's brain. When PJ spends long, boring hours stuck in a car on a surveillance job, she amuses herself by counting all the places on her body where she can stash her gun – she's up to twelve now – and she wishes to thank Lynne for the idea. It helps to make up for the indignity of having to pee into a one-pound coffee can.

About This Book

IN THIS SEQUEL TO *Hell On Heels,* PJ Santini uncovers the shocking truth about her late husband, a secret that places her in grave danger. Danger of death by *fettuccini Alfredo*, danger of trusting the wrong man, danger of an actual terrifying end to her life. Fortunately, she is armed with a good family, decent common sense, and a spectacular set of 38 DD's.

For my hero
Chuck
Today, tomorrow, always

HEELS OF FORTUNE

LYNNE RUSSELL

Sequel to the
#1 PJ Santini Adventure
HELL ON HEELS

CHAPTER ONE

"I weel suck on your poosy until your ears flaap like those of an elephant!" the deep voice intoned over bump-n-grind background music that bore a striking resemblance to Hockey Night In Canada. The call was coming from my parents' house.

"Nonna, is that you? Hello, Nonna Giovanna? Why are you calling, are you alright?"

"*Aspetta*, wait... no no, not you my love..." she said to the man at her end, then the line went dead. My transplanted Sicilian grandmother was discovering amateur dubbed-in American porn, and the family was trembling at the possibilities.

That's what you get for answering the phone in church, I told myself. But it was the other call that really started the trouble. It came so soon, I thought it was Nonna again.

"Not now. I'll call you back," I whispered.

"You have something that doesn't belong to you. I want it."

"Excuse me?" The last time somebody said that to me, it was that bitch Kathy Shula in the parking lot during Senior Prom, trying to repossess the captain of the hockey team. She'd been way overreacting. I was only borrowing him.

"I'll put it in short headlines, so you can understand," he said dryly. "Your husband thought there was only the Polaroid. But there's a cod, a memory cod. You give me the goose, I'll give you the cod."

"Cod. Is this about fish?"

"The carrrd, the memory carrrd!"

"Oh, *carrrd*. Are you from Boston? Who is this? Is this that 1-900-SexTalk number I accidentally dialed last week? You know it's illegal to keep calling me back."

"Remember, you're in the picture, too. If you don't give me the goose, the cod will go to your friends at the Precinct, and I promise you, it will take... you... down. You'll never know what hit you. You have 48 hours. I'll be in touch."

"Wait! What am I, a farmer? I don't have any goose. You have the wrong number."

"No I don't, Ms. Santini, I'm looking right at you."

"Who *are* you?" I demanded, whipping around, craning my neck to search faces. Nobody was looking at me, and nobody was nobody was on a cell phone. The guy had hung up. About that time, the church minister walked to center front, stretched out his arms, bent his knees, and made palms-down movements, his eyes fixed on some distant, imaginary chopper he was guiding in for a landing. This being a room full of TV people, it takes more than that to shut us up. So he lifted his arms out to his sides, about shoulder height, and began flapping in slow motion like an Animal Kingdom lake bird. The effect was curious enough that people did start paying attention. And snickering.

We had gathered there to bury our own twisted television colleague, Gerald Sigmund, "Siggy", who'd been running a monster drug and prostitution ring off of his humble newsroom computer. It had gotten him dead. I'd become involved in that case both as a reporter and as a private investigator, but all that was finished now. The only things that were left were spent bullet casings from one end of Buffalo to the other, and glass shards that I was still pulling out of my head from a terrifying episode in a strip joint dressing room.

Droplets of perspiration were running through the expensive M*A*C foundation on my upper lip, which did not improve my mood. The stranger on the phone had made me feel really pissy. It's not good to feel pissy at a funeral. So I leaned to my right and decided to take it out on another of his gender.

"Pssst, hey. It's sweltering in here! Was it absolutely necessary for me to wear all this bedroomy crap?" I complained into the man's smooth, tan cheek. I watched the back of his hand slide up and down my arm, and it gave me the shivers, the sort of shivers that make your pupils dilate and drool slide out the corners of your mouth.

"All I suggested was the color," he said without looking. "Two layers of lace and long sleeves was *your* idea. So then, take one of them off."

"Smartass. You know the bottom one is underwear. This was all I had in black. Except for my Catwoman outfit, which would've set the pews on fire."

I didn't think people had to wear black to funerals anymore, but when have I ever said no to Tango Daly, the architect and owner of Iroquois Investigations, and the hottest private detective boss on the planet? Alright, I have, but it's torture every time. So I've developed a hard and fast rule about hard, fast ones like Daly: When I start fantasizing about a possible future, any possible future, I picture myself a year down the road, seven months pregnant, standing in a pink terrycloth robe and fuzzy scuffs in a laundry room, spot-cleaning his Jockeys. I'm allergic to that. But then my little internal voice starts up. *You know if it were Daly, you'd like it. He'd have you propped up on the washer, diddling your spin cycle, and then...* then I tell the bitch to shut up.

My name is PJ Santini. As my full name is pure Italian linguistic pandemonium - Pompeo Jiacobbe Santini, after my grandfather, according to some secret family tradition - I just go by PJ, or sometimes friends call me Janice, or my relatives go with Pommie, which is worse than the original.

The scene of the crime, and love is always a crime, is Buffalo, New York. I'm a decent private detective, and a better television news reporter. Most of the time it's hard to concentrate, because I'm hanging onto life by my fingernails. What with juggling relationships, wacko blood relatives and revolving charge payments, the one thing that calms me is my eight-by-ten-foot walk-in closet. I've got it lined with magnificent high heels. I've arranged them by color, and illuminated them with the biggest, bitchinest crystal chandelier I could afford. It is without a doubt the best-organized part of my entire life. When Nonna sees the shoes, especially the boots with the thin heels, she spits and calls them slut shoes. Then she does one of those dramatic two-way over-the-shoulder glances to see if anybody's watching, and of course no one ever is, and she wants to know what size I wear. Thank god I'm into a 10, twice the size that supports her 4 foot 11-1/2 inch frame.

Speaking of numbers, I just had a birthday and would rather not talk about age. Okay, thirty-something, but that's it. I've decided age is only a number, and mine is unlisted. When anybody asks, I've got a rehearsed answer that works for me. I just say I think of myself as a well-maintained, midrange convertible that's just out of warranty. Nice paint, a few dings, substantial bucket seats. Buffed up and durable, in Pop's vernacular, but still fun to drive and ready for action.

So there I sat in the crowded church, squished against Daly, wondering about the telephone mystery man who wanted so badly for me to goose him. Daly's thighs felt solid in his expensive Italian slacks, and he smelled faintly of a heady mix of gun oil, mystery and power.

On my other side was Johnny Renza, a fellow journalist and the first boy who ever loved me – literally. His hormones shifted into overdrive in junior high, almost overnight. One day he was childishly walking through the cafeteria at lunch, "blessing" our open cartons of milk with a crucifix that was dropping salt tablets out of a secret compartment underneath; the next day we were making out in the confessional. Wild and charismatic, he was different from the others, more willing to take chances.

In the years that followed, somehow he was always in my life. Then at college, one starlit night in his car, he undid my bra with an impressive flourish and pointed out that we'd known each other for so long, he'd actually watched me grow up. At that moment, I realized in a rare flash of insight that I couldn't honestly say the same thing about him. He hadn't grown up at all, and I didn't think he ever would. So I started looking around for more mature candidates. Before long, I snagged myself Lou Bonmarito, a law school grad. Much to my family's delight, he asked me to marry him and I said okay. Ma and Pop cheerfully cleaned out their Pommie's Wedding Savings Account, which had been accruing interest ten years longer than they'd thought it would, and the family threw a big Sicilian blowout with dreams of grandchildren dancing in their heads.

Forty-eight hours later, Lou was dead. A damn heart attack on our honeymoon. You can't make this shit up.

These days, the men in my life are the ones I work with. Including Renza, who also went to journalism school and is a fellow reporter at my Buffalo television station. His beat is crime. My beat is anything they'll give me. My work is every bit as good as his, and more than once my intelligence, intuition, and certain other body parts have outpaced him in getting a story. But that same female equipment also gets me the dopey assignments, while he enjoys the challenging ones. He does it by bluffing.

Just look at him. Renza is the only person I know who could get away with wearing a white linen suit to a funeral that isn't in the Bahamas. He has everybody snowed. Women fall all over him because of his dark, wavy hair and big, moony Italian eyes; men wish they could manufacture the same cocky attitude and trademark look. Renza. Johnny Renza.

"Check it out," he whispered to me, angling his head toward the gaggle of plainclothes, gum-chewing cops collected in the side doorway of the church. "They even brought long lenses."

"Why are they here?" I asked him.

"They're Longoria's eyes and ears. You'll notice the bastard's not here himself, but he wants to make sure we're all behaving."

Frank Longoria is another guy I grew up with, a juvenile delin-quent-turned-Senior Homicide Detective. I know where his skeletons are buried, and he knows I know it. But when I reported on our infamous recent shoot-out during the final phase of the Gerald Sigmund case, I couldn't tell it all. I'd had to leave out Frank's connection to The Mob, because I couldn't exactly prove it.

He wanted to keep it that way. His boys would be busy taking notes today, for purposes of intimidation and possible retribution. Not just with me, but with anybody on the guest list, and the guest list looked like a Who's Who of *Criminal Minds*.

Eventually we adjourned to our cars and made the drive to the Olde Town Cemetery. It occurred to me that this was the one time we knew beyond a shadow of a doubt, after slippery Siggy's Central American drug operation finally blew up, exactly where the elusive creep really was. Every car in the funeral procession had its air conditioning jacked up in the stifling summer heat as we snaked along Remembrance Way, which ironically had been named for veterans of foreign wars, not foreign scores. After a couple of turns, we parked and made the uncomfortable walk to the grave.

The hot ground by the casket sucked up my black patent leather stilettos like soft cement. Sweat trailed down the center of my back, as I made an unsteady effort to shift my weight without leaning on either Daly or Renza. Both would consider that foreplay.

An hour later, we'd wrapped it up and everybody was grateful to be headed out, when a guy shouted over from three tombstones away.

"Hey! Do I look crazy to you?" I wouldn't say his eyes were spinning around like Marty Feldman's, but it was hard to tell which one was looking at me.

"That would depend on your definition of crazy," I told him.

"They're trying to make me believe I'm insane, but I'm as solid as you are."

As me? That would be a problem. "How can you tell?" I shouted back. "Everybody who's crazy swears they're not."

He dragged his shovel over and leaned an elbow on it, while he wiped sweat out of his eyes with the back of his other hand.

"Well, I know what I know. I dug my ass off last night getting a plot ready for today, and today the damn thing isn't here. It's gone."

"Are you telling me somebody stole a hole? Are you a gravedigger?"

"Cemetery maintenance specialist. Willy Short's the name. I use a machine for most of it, then I finish it off myself. Last night I dug it, today it's solid ground with three inches of grass growing on it. Wanna see?"

"Uh, no." By now Renza had bailed - the chickenshit - and Daly had backed off to enjoy the show. Turns out Willy Short had been digging alone in the moonlight, and his only companion was *Evan Williams Kentucky Straight*, not what you'd call a reliable witness. Still, when he came-to in his own bed this morning, his overalls had new dirt on them, just as you'd expect from someone who'd been digging.

"This isn't the first time. Say, you're on TV, aren't you? Will you explain to my boss it's not my fault? Now there's no place to bury Lola."

Everything in me said *Get out while you can!* But I could not help myself. "Okay, Mr. Short, I'll bite. Who's Lola?"

"That's cute, 'I'll bite'. Lola can't bite anymore. She's a Schnoodle. Or she was."

"What's a Schnoodle, some religious sect?"

"It's a sort of a hypoallergenic cross between a Schnauzer and a Poodle. Over there, across that row of hydrangeas, in the pet cemetery."

That was it. Purely out of habit, I lobbed an Iroquois Investigations business card at him - I sure didn't want him calling me at the station - and took a fisted swipe at Tango, who was standing there grinning with his arms crossed. As usual, he was faster and caught my wrist before I could do any real damage; also as usual, I couldn't wait to try it again later. There was something about the way the breeze caught his shirt, the way the black silk settled over his toned chest... it made my head fizzy.

"Want a ride?" he said seductively as he strode easily beside me. His ride was a fancy BMW 700 series command post. A black stealthmobile that housed every piece of covert operations equipment that wasn't already in his two-story, locked-down private office. I wasn't positive how he got the name Tango; but I knew he'd been US Army Special Forces, had done unspecified covert work afterward, and had enough martial arts expertise to slice you like bacon. I was glad I was his friend. An enemy would have a bad day.

"Very funny", I told him over my shoulder. He knew my ride was still the Toad, a pathetic, worn, green automobile the insurance company had generously loaned me when my pet, mint-condition silver Mercedes SLK, named Sweet Boy, had been ripped off right under my nose. But I'd never given up hope: around every corner, in every parking lot, I expected to see Sweet Boy again, and I wasn't going to settle for buying anything else. The Toad accepted that he was only a temp and took me downtown anyway, to my condo in Erie Towers on Lakefront Boulevard.

This former marital love nest was now pricey and refinanced, but I did have that glamorous minimum wage television job, along with spotty private eye assignments. Besides, the mortgage company and I have a special, environmentally-conscious understanding about late payments: I don't burn unnecessary fuel driving around town to find more work, and they save trees by simply emailing me the routine foreclosure notices.

I used the condominium Electropass to open the underground garage gate, and swiped it again to take the elevator to the sixth floor. I really appreciated living in a secure building. I needed all the distance I could put between myself and obsessed newscast viewers who were convinced we had a meaningful relationship. Like the IRS Tax Examiner who, according to the IRS's own Internal Investigations department, had actually set up an "altar" to me in his apartment.

"But don't worry about it," they said, "it's just a little altar."

"Oh really? Then why did you come to me? Why are you telling me this? Why did go into his house?" No answer. But it didn't stop there. The jackass shot out one of my tires on the expressway and then, when I pulled over to phone for help, he pulled in behind me and asked, all innocent and helpful, if there was anything he could do. What he didn't know was that my friends at CID, Criminal Investigations at the police department, pulled the file they already had on him and easily ID'd him for me. It put him back on their radar, and on my ever-growing shit list. And that was just the latest stalker.

I exited the elevator onto my floor, and tried again to fall in love with the purple-flecked orange industrial carpet the Condominium Association had insisted on putting in. It looked like fresh chopped prunes in orange juice, and so much like somebody had just thrown it up, that you'd constantly run the toe of your shoe over it to see if it smeared. The configuration of the carpeted landing was square; each floor had four pretty big corner apartments. The area was deserted and the air was stuffy, as I turned the key in my lock. It felt so good to step into the security of my living room, and breathe in the rush of fresh air off Lake Erie. It would have felt a lot better, if I'd actually been the one to have left the sliding glass balcony doors open.

Someone was here! I swung inside, hugged the foyer wall and pulled out Daisy, my trusty Sig-Sauer P230. She lives in a black nylon holster strapped to my thigh, with a little pink ribbon bow sewn on the snap.

I began a room-by-room search. Living room. Dining room. Kitchen. All clear. I could see most of the bedroom reflected in the mirrors of its sliding closet doors, so I wheeled in and brought the muzzle of the gun in line with the center of the bathroom. Nothing. Maybe I really did forget to close the balcony doors. Still, the texture of the place had changed. Things seemed, well, off. Someone had been here, I was sure . Just as I'd felt it the day I came home from my husband's funeral. Both times, a person would have known exactly where I was, and that there was no way I'd be home unexpectedly.

But what could anyone possibly want? That first time, I'd been too shocked to think about it. I'd become a widow just two days after I'd become a wife. I admit relationships can have a shelf life when you really get into them, but this one hadn't even been opened all the way.

I holstered Daisy and kicked off my heels, then flopped down on the bed and wiggled out of everything else. The nice thing about living on the sixth floor in a condo that faces Lake Erie is that you can walk around in the buff with the drapes open anytime you want. And this time I really wanted. I detoured to the kitchen for a glass of Chianti, and took my time ambling toward the balcony, digging my toes into the soft, champagne-colored carpet. The feeling of the air on my body reminded me how unfair it was that men could go topless in public, and women couldn't. I took another slow sip, roughing up my long, frizzy red hair, thinking I had a decent shot at looking hot if I had to. At that exact moment, a savage the size of a Kodak bear in a dark ski mask came charging off the balcony and body checked me.

"Wha...! Uuuff......!" The blow knocked the breath right out of me and slammed me into the drywall. I could feel the coolness of the paint against my back as I slid down to the floor. An electric wave swept through my limbs, along with the chilling revelation that I was completely helpless, and at someone else's mercy. The last thing I remember before everything went white was the sound of his voice as he made tracks for the door.

"Nice tits, sweetheart."

By the time I came around, the red wine had soaked into my beautiful light carpet, and summer storm clouds had gathered on the lake. I was still lying there in the nude, in plain view of a wide open front door. The drywall had a good-sized dent in it, shaped like my head. I didn't know whether to be enormously relieved it was over, or pissed off. On the one hand, this jackass had executed a home invasion. When they do that, they're usually prepared to deal with you. If I had surprised him on the balcony, I shuddered to think of what might have happened. I could've been tossed overboard. On the other hand, under the circumstances, my being naked and hot and all, he'd run like hell and hadn't even tried anything funny. True, he did compliment my girls, but that was more of an afterthought. I would not want this to get out.

My hands trembled as I crawled to the telephone table and used the land line Daly made me put in, for security and message capability, he said. The 800 number all of Daly's investigators use was on speed dial for just such emergencies.

"Operations," he answered on the third ring.

"It's me! Somebody broke into my apartment and knocked me out!"

"And?"

"And what?"

"What did he do?" Tango asked deliberately. I could imagine the set of his jaw, his knuckles turning white as he held the phone. He was my number one protector.

"He didn't do anything... at least I don't think he did."

"Don't you know?" His voice eased. "Do you need a hospital?"

"No, I just don't know how he got in or what he wanted."

"Get out of there immediately, PJ, we don't know what he might have left there."

"Left? Like what?"

"Like anything. Cameras, snakes..." *Snakes?*

"I can't."

"Why not?"

"'I'll have to put on some clothes back on, first."

Silence.

"Let me get this straight," he said, and I could hear the corners of his mouth curling. "An intruder brazenly risks detection, breaks in and lies in wait for you. You come home. You take off all your clothes. He sees this, and he runs." This was not going the way I thought it would.

"Something like that."

"You will never live this down. Further, I will sacrifice the rest of my busy day to help you get over any feelings of rejection or inadequacy. I'll be right over." And he would, too. I could spend from now until tomorrow feeling a whole lot better... safe and satisfied. But then I wouldn't ever want him to leave, and I've got that thing about the laundry room.

"Oh, no you don't. The day has gone to shit, but I'm still due in the newsroom, overdue in fact. If I don't show, they don't write the damn checks." While most days I'd rather get laid than paid, there *were* the bills to think of.

But first, I wanted to know how that thug had gotten in. So I blew a kiss to Daly, dragged myself to my feet, and locked the door. Then I called down to Security – and I use the term loosely. Javier Calderon was employed there only because the Erie Towers Condominium Board of Directors' sole requirements were that he have vital signs, work cheap, and be able to answer the phone in English during commercial breaks on the television at the concierge desk. At present, he was working exhausting twelve-hour shifts, so I could lay the blame on him for practically anything that went wrong.

"Javier, sorry to interrupt *The Price Is Right*, but there was a man in my apartment today."

"Yes, Miss PJ."

"Did you know that?"

"Yes, Miss PJ."

"How did he get into the elevator, much less into my home?"

"He was your brother."

"He was *not* my brother. This is the third time this has happened, and you know none of them has been my brother. It can't happen again!"

"Yes, Miss PJ. *Oh...Iha! Fifteen hundred for the washer/dryer!*"

I bit my lip and slammed down the phone, and went to find some clothes; at least *that* I could control. I always reach for the shoes first, and the rest just seems to take care of itself. As I wanted authoritative shoes with bitchin' attitude, there could be only one choice: red Mary Janes with four-inch heels. God bless Mary Janes, they're too innocent to be so hot, especially in red. Black pencil skirt, stretchy white-collared shirt with French cuffs and a short string of real pearls. It shouts "I've just escaped from the convent and need to learn the ways of the world!"

CHAPTER TWO

I took Lakeshore out and this time followed Skyler Rd, not liking to use the same route twice in a row, and made a hard right into the TV station parking lot. There was something reassuring about seeing Renza's car there. Even though I wanted to kill him on a routine basis, we did have a lot of history together. His '99 white Ford sedan sat at the far end. He thought it was important for an investigative reporter to drive a forgettable car. I, of course, had him beat on that score with the Toad.

When I turned in to park, I saw his sedan was cozied up against a brand new, bright red BMW Z4 convertible. This could mean only one thing: Kathy Shula. Alleged journalist and professional blonde bitch since we were in Catholic school in our Italian-Polish neighborhood of Lovejoy. Her very presence had torpedoed my happy moments, from Huggies to husband. I suspected, but couldn't confirm, that away from the newsroom Renza was routinely and unselfishly easing her through the difficult challenges of writing complete sentences, much as he did in high school. I didn't know why I should care; he'd become community property when I threw him back into the pond and got married, but it still pissed me off.

I went in the employee entrance and tiptoed down the hall, no point in drawing attention on a workday, and moved past the room where I make my most important telephone calls and come up with the best ideas: the bathroom. Before I could fish out my office keys, Murray Soper, the news director, nailed me. My latest stories were on his greatest hits list – murder, drugs, prostitution – and in spite of his de-meaning attitude toward women in the newsroom, they had won me some respect. Never mind that I practically needed a crowbar to get paychecks out of him.

"Santini. Nice of you to stop by. Over here, right now," he wheezed and blew a big one into his wrinkled plaid handkerchief. Half the news-room scrambled to cover up their drinks. He made a sweeping gesture toward the big Dry Erase board on the wall by the assignment desk.

"I'd like to acquaint you with a little procedural thing," he said, sar-casm being his middle name. "This is called the Assignment Board. On it, you will find the slugs for today's stories, together with the reporters' and photogs' names, the story locations and the newscasts in which the stories will run. Also, there's a place to note progress on the stories. As you can see, more than half of them are finished. Take a good look. There's even one for you. Look closer. Can you see what's missing?"

I made a big show of squinting at the board. "Nope, not me. Nice job, Murray, it's all good."

The tittering began behind the computers, and Murray gave it a beat. The handkerchief slid around his scalp, trying but failing to ab-sorb one more drop of sweat. As he barely came up to my shoulder when I wasn't even wearing heels, I got a satellite's view of his matted combover. I hoped I would live long enough to forget it. He shoved a paper at me and retreated to his office, to peer out into the newsroom and survey the damage through his Venetian blinds. He'd scribbled down my assignment, and it was not at all what I expected after my big recent stories:

Santini/Smith: Report on the sad economic state of individual taxpayers who have to sell their houses. I want this to be a tear jerker. Be careful, it wasn't easy to line this one up, nobody wants to talk about hard times. See Delia Minsky, 24 Macduff Lane. *NOW!*

"Oh c'mon, Murray, what the fuck!" I kept talking at him as the blinds slowly closed. "Give me a break! Tearjerker? I'm a damn good reporter, and you know it! When Renza goes out he takes an ankle holster, and when I go out I take Kleenex. Who's got the challenge, here?" Renza shot me a sorry-about-that look, and I tried hard not to flip him off. After all, it wasn't his fault.

But Kathy, who was perched next to him, didn't look so sorry. I acted like I didn't see her, and the barely concealed bazookas she was aiming at him. I was pretty sure she blew her whole clothing allowance at Sluts R Us. I've been known to pick up a few corsets, myself; the difference is, I don't wear mine on the outside.

"So, Johnny, what are you working on today, besides our cub reporter?" I said across the newsroom.

"Oh, nothin' extra. Just your average body turning up in your average neighborhood." He downplayed it so I wouldn't get upset. Well, it was too late.

"A body? Oh, no problem, probably too boring to take up your time. A rose-snipping accident that led to a fatal hangnail, not much of a story." My voice was rising. "Then a small whirlwind came along," I made a motion like I was stirring a cake, "and it innocently dusted the remains with layers of dirt, and there they lay for ten years, maybe longer." I went soprano, and people were turning to watch. "Then one day a heavy rain washed it all away and exposed the body. Little children skipping hand-in-hand on their way to school made the grisly discovery, and they immediately Tweeted it to the rest of humanity, and now poor Johnny has to cover it. You're right, my story is so much more stimulating!"

"C'mon, Smitty," I said to my photographer. "Let's get the hell outta here."

Smitty, who was always on some diet or other, had switched to the sugar diet. This way he didn't have to worry about his glucose level dropping precipitously half an hour after he ate a donut, because he was always eating. He stashed a bag of *Brach's* Bon-Bons in his camera bag and we scampered out to his van.

24 Macduff Lane was a small, well-tended periwinkle blue clapboard house with a brilliant array of colorful flowers along the front walk. It was in a block of old fashioned houses, all with garages set back a few feet. Properties were separated by chain link fences. The rear yard was filled with an unruly English garden of perennials of every description. They looked aggressively healthy.

I went to meet Delia Minsky on the front porch, while Smitty got some cover video of the outside. Delia was about forty years old and my height, 5'9". Medium build, a woman Pop would call not chubby but "well fed". She wore denim jeans with a man's shirt over, and the very ideas of mascara and root touchup were foreign to her. Good teeth, nice handshake. Social, but not really warm. Who cared, I wasn't going to date her, just do a story on her house.

"This won't take long, will it?" she said. "We expected you earlier. Can I get you something to drink?"

"No thanks, we're kind of in a hurry, too. So you're looking to sell your place."

"Yes, and probably at a loss. The house is in good shape, but we just can't deal with taxes and maintenance and repairs anymore." She looked nervous.

"By "we", you mean you and your husband?"

"No, me and my brother. Cornelius."

I took notes and kept asking. "What do you and your brother do?"

"I don't do much of anything, except plant things, that's always been my passion. He's a photographer, but he's semi-retired. Got sick a few years ago, then he got better. He just never got back to work."

"I see." I played with my pen and tried to drum up some sympathy and a tearjerker of a story for these two, who were not at all the struggling, hardworking, down-on-their-luck couple I'd expected. The story just wasn't coming. Smitty gave me a "Why are we here?" look. I shrugged back.

"I just want to say I've worked really hard on the gardens," she finally offered, "and the new owners have got to sign a statement that they'll leave them exactly as they are, no changes of any kind. They've been certified as a Wildlife Habitat. It's very important. Everything you see is there for a reason: animal food, shelter, all of it."

"I'm sure it is," I told her. "Mind if I have a look around?" She took me through the small rooms, and then we came to a closed door. "What's in here?" I asked.

"Not what... who. It's Cornelius," she said as she swung the door open and the sound of the television drowned out everything she said next.

"Hello dear, how are you?" Delia shouted. "These nice people are doing a news story to help us sell the house."

Cornelius, all three hundred pounds of him, was hooked up to a plastic tube that floated O^2 past his nose. He twisted around in his cordovan pseudo-suede La-Z-Boy, and exhaled a lungful of green cigar smoke. "Piss off," he said to his sister. Then he leveled his gaze at me. "You, too."

She closed the door. "That went well. He's between Island Paradise cruises, and he gets real testy. When he got sick, he was all set to die; but then he didn't, and now we've all got to live with it."

"Isn't it dangerous to smoke around oxygen?" I asked, backing down the hall.

"He usually turns it off first."

Holllleeee shit. See, this is why I never, ever would have wanted to become a real estate agent, having to meet up with wack jobs in strange locations... and fifty percent of them are your own clients. No, wait, that's the PI business.

"What will you do when you sell?" I asked her.

"I'll leave. Everything stays. I'm already packed."

Suddenly I wanted to help this woman, who clearly had issues with asserting herself. If Cornelius were my brother, I'd leave him, too.

"Just one last question, Delia. What can I do to help you, er, move on? What have you not told me?"

She frowned. "Oh yes, how could I have forgotten? The view from upstairs, it's terrific. Trees all the way up the street." She pulled down the attic stairs in the hallway. "When I was a kid I would go up there. Don't mind the mess; in order to show the house, I dumped a lot of junk on its way to the trash next week." She checked her watch. "Oh my," she said, "I've got to be someplace. You just take a look around and then close the door behind you, okay?"

I assured her I'd only be a couple more minutes, not having a strong desire to end my days mingling my DNA with Cornelius's. I imagined the two of us in an apocalyptic, cigar-sparked explosion, with charred globules of our bodies raining down as green fallout. Smitty and his famous survival instinct were already outside. The climb to the attic was an adventure, in my straight skirt and Mary Janes, but I did okay. I didn't rip, run or wrench anything. And Delia was right: the view was gorgeous, maybe the best thing about the house. Somebody could stick an office up here – or a recalcitrant relative.

Which brought to mind Cornelius. Had he always been such a pain in the ass? What was his story? A photographer with an attitude like that wouldn't make much money in the real world. On the way out of the attic, I couldn't resist moving a few things around. There was roller skating equipment, although I saw no other evidence of children. It would be hard to imagine either one of them wading into the murky waters of romance and child rearing. There were a few sealed boxes. Another was open and in the junk pile, and it held books: an old almanac, a volume of ghost stories, a small journal. As Delia obviously no longer had an interest in these things, and Cornelius already had told me where to get off, I debated whether it would be ethical – or even a service to humanity - to pocket the journal as a sort of, you know, archeological... preservationist....

Oh hell, I stuffed it in my purse.

Smitty was waiting way out in the street with the camera, ready for my standup. He waved the mike. "Hurry up, PJ. This place could blow any minute. Where've you been?"

"Research. I need to stand on the lawn for this one, could you come in a little? If you don't, you'll be so far away I'll have to use signal flags." He didn't budge, and maybe he had a point. So I did it from the curb.

He counted me down, "Five, four, three..." then he switched to hand signals for two and one, and cued me with a nice sweep of his index finger, and I began.

"Many families are feeling enough of an economic pinch to give up the expenses of ownership, to become renters instead. Or some are moving in with relatives. Others are simply moving on. For every *SOLD* sign, there is an owner walking away from more than the rest of us can possibly imagine. PJ Santini for Your Buffalo News." That ought to do it.

As Smitty stashed the cords and tripod in the van and I climbed back in, I had a second thought. "Let's swing by Property Records at the courthouse before we go back."

"Why, don't you think she owns the house?"

"Just want to be sure. See the sign? They call it a FISBO – For Sale By Owner. If she'd listed it with an agent, the brokerage would have checked out the ownership, first thing. I just want to be on the safe side."

"Okay. Be sure to say hi to Over for me."

Over is Smitty's nickname for my primary source at the Erie County Clerk's Office. She really goes by Turner. No first name, just Turner. She's tiny and skinny as a rail, with minimal butt and boobs and absolutely straight brown hair that's all one length, like Cousin It. It falls down in front of her face when she's working. I don't know how any light gets in there. On a date – and our own beefy Smitty's been out with her – a guy might have a hard time figuring out which is the front and which is the back. Hence, the name he came up with, Turner Over.

"HI, PJ," TURNER SAID with a pencil in her mouth. "Whaddaya got for me today?"

"Delia Minsky, or maybe Cornelius Minsky, 24 Macduff Lane. Any way you want it." Five minutes later, she was back with two printouts.

"Delia came up. Ran it both ways, did searches by name and by property address. Take 'em both."

"Thanks. You're wonderful."

"I know." She pulled her hair back behind her ears and flashed me an unexpected movie star smile. "Then why does Smitty tease me so much?"

"He likes you."

"Well," she waved a left hand with an empty third finger and sang, "If he likes it he shoulda put a ring on it!"

"I'll be sure to tell him," I said with a wink, and left with the goods. Having a contact in Property Records is like dating a guy who reps couture clothes. What they give you costs them nothing, they make you happy, and everybody gets high on beating the system.

Back at the station, I couldn't get past the feeling that Delia didn't seem all that sad to be leaving her home; but I wrote the story Murray wanted and gave the copy to Smitty anyway, so he could edit the video to it.

My body was aching from being slammed into the wall, and I just wanted to go home. I dropped the Minskys' pilfered journal into the trunk of the car, and started driving.

The Toad maneuvered along on autopilot, as I puzzled over some thought that was trying to elbow its way to the front of my brain. What was it? The phone call in church had been bothering me. That man. He said Cod. Card. Cod. A Boston accent, if ever there was one. Who else had I talked with from Boston today? Someone... or had I heard a voice on radio, or television? That sound, that voice...

And then it hit me. It wasn't what he'd said, but *the way* he'd said it: "Nice tits, sweethot." I slammed on the brakes, and the Toad fishtailed to a stop.

CHAPTER THREE

Javier Calderon's lapels were stretching and the stitches were popping as I gripped his concierge jacket with my fists. *"What did he look like? What?"*

He choked, and the grease on his sideburns began to slip. "He look like all your brothers, Miss PJ. They all very handsome men." He tried a smile.

"Let me." Tango moved smoothly around to the concierge desk and positioned himself between us, his arms held loosely in front of him with fingertips barely touching, as he prepared for any eventuality. His voice was cool and quiet.

"Hello, Mr. Calderon, my name is Tango Daly. Unlike Ms. Santini, I am not your friend. I've been researching you. I know why you left your job at the ketchup factory. Although I don't know what you thought you were going to do with a half-ton U-Haul filled with stolen *Buffalo Wings Hot 'n' Heavy* sauce - we'll get to that later. Now I have two words for you," he spoke them slowly and clearly, "Green Card." Javier swallowed hard. "Your thirty seconds begins..." Daly looked at his watch "...now."

A flood of words spilled from Javier's mouth. "Blond hair, brown eyes, mustache, mole under the left eye, about five foot eleven, big hands."

"Scars or tattoos?"

"Not that I could see."

"Thank you," Daly said.

"You welcome." Javier stood transfixed and terrified as we turned to leave.

"By the way, Mr. Calderon, how much money was he flashing, in those big hands of his?"

"Fifty dollars."

"Let me see it." Calderon fished a nice, crisp new bill out of the side pocket of his navy Erie Towers blazer, and handed it over.

Daly tucked it in my bra. "Buy yourself something I'll like." To Javier he said, "I would have held out for a hundred."

So, we knew what the intruder looked like, and that he and the caller were the same person. He was a New Englander. With 14 million people claiming that distinction, it wasn't very much to go on. Daly, of course, considered it a lead.

I spent the rest of evening sipping champagne out of the bottle through a straw, sitting Indian style on the rug in my walk-in, among my friends The Shoes, wondering if everybody's life was as screwed up as mine. I put some effort into contemplating what naughty and patently irresponsible thing I should do with the fifty. When I woke up at 2 a.m. with the imprint of the carpet on my cheek, I'd been having another hot Napoleon Solo shoe salesman dream. "Come with me," I told the dapper, handsome, knowing Man From U.N.C.L.E., half asleep as I maneuvered over to the bed, "and bring those sparkly pink Betsey Johnson heels, the ones with the ankle strap and the big bow on the toe." He hardly ever says anything, but his movements are fraught with meaning. Real shoe salesmen these days just don't get it. I tucked myself in bed and went back to sleep. Napoleon always caresses the top of my instep like he's petting a wild animal into submission, then he pulls the shoe out of its tissue and presents it for my approval. His big brown eyes never leave mine. I simply nod, massaging his short hair.

Why Napoleon Solo, you ask? Because he's smart and sexy and trained to do things he can't talk about, and his other girlfriend will never interrupt us by texting him on his personal iPhone, because he's Old School and never even heard of that.

"Downtown," he said. He spoke! What did you say, Napoleon? He said it again. "DOWN-town!" This could be the ticket to the next level of our relationship! You want to go downtown? Now? "DOWN-town!" It came again, and Napoleon began to fade. My answerphone was screening an incoming call, and the volume was all the way up.

"I took-a him DOWN-town! We gotta talk! We need a sit-down, pronto!" It was Nonna Giovanna. Pop's mother's English language skills are a combination of various home shopping channel Florentine Gold jewelry shows, *The Sopranos,* and whichever movie she's watching today.

"No, wait," I pleaded with Napoleon, "don't go!" He smiled wistfully, tilted his head, checked his watch, and vanished. Damn it! She calls at a time like this? We were just getting to know each other.

"Pommie, it's the cat burglar! You got a problem with pickin' it the hell up? I can guarantee you the closest shave you'll ever know!" Oh dear god, she's gotten her hands on a *Sweeney Todd* DVD. I could hear Pop in the background, grappling with her for the handset.

"Aw geez, I told her not to call you so early!" he shouted. "I told her you can't even find your feet before ten." I looked at the little crystal clock by the bed. It said 7:30. I hit the speakerphone button.

"What's goin' on?" I mumbled.

"We had an attempted robbery last night," Pop said. "Some idiot while your Ma and I were at Bingo. Your Nonna clocked him good." Pop was a cop for decades and he likes nothing better than a mystery. He and his buddies run a damned successful Cold Case outfit on their tight retirement incomes, down in the basement. It's his one chance to voice complete thoughts in a house where he can't shoehorn a word in sideways, between his wife and his mother. Besides solving old cases, mealtime is Pop's biggest event, and he makes sure nothing gets in the way.

"I'll be right over," I told him.

I threw on jeans, a grey Buffalo Sabres *Hockey is the Most Fun You Can Have With Your Clothes On* tank top and my Italian *Scarpa "Mojito"* athletic shoes. Then, because attitude is everything, I pulled out Prada sunglasses and put my empty wallet in a matching Louis Vuitton clutch. The car was running on fumes, so I stopped for gas.

Big mistake without coffee. I stood stupidly at the pump, aiming the nozzle at the car and wondering what had happened to the gas tank. Then I realized the tank was on the other side. So I got back in and drove around, and backed up to another pump. It was still on the wrong side. Two construction jockeys in a big navy pickup truck were leaning out to watch. One of them smirked, "A redhead. An' you thought it was just blondes." Another guy got out of his car and walked over. He said to look at the Toad's gas gauge, because there's always an arrow that tells you on which side of the car you'll find the tank door. I played dumb like I'd never driven the car before, and said thanks.

I got back in, drove forward, then backed up to the next row of pumps, and still got it wrong. He pointed that out, and I said the first thing that came to mind.

"I didn't really want gas. I'm here to practice parallel parking." If my luck held, I could make it to a station near my parents' place in Lovejoy.

Every time I drive into the neighborhood where I grew up, I think of it as what the Italians and Poles who settled it called it: Iron Island. It's surrounded by railroad tracks. It never was the most elegant part of town, just working class with real values that stay with you all your life. When I'm having a bad day or am about to, like right now, this is a very grounding thought. I took Broadway and pointed the Toad toward Casanova.

All the way over, I imagined a burglar coming face to face with Nonna, and wishing to god he were dead. You can take the girl out of Sicily, but it ends there. The woman can be terrifying. Height: short enough to be too short to go on half the rides at the Erie County Fair.

Hair: frizzy ear-length salt and pepper, cut like her head was in a colander and some drunk used pinking shears to clip the stragglers. Deceptively agile in her black dress, black shawl, black opaque stockings and black Oxfords - black combat boots after Labor Day. Now that she was in the States, she lusted after the shotguns she and the other widows used to pack for protection in the Old Country. Instead, she learned to swing a baseball bat like a Bruce Lee *escrima* stick. Somewhere in Buffalo this morning, there was a wasted housebreaker whimpering like a little girl and licking his wounds. I parked the car on the curb outside the family house, and could hear the racket all the way from the sidewalk.

"Oh J.M.J.!" That was my brother, Tony, who'd learned early on from Pop that males in that household can never underestimate the value of getting it said fast, even if you have to abbreviate it: J.M.J. is short for Jesus Mary and Joseph, the classic Catholic substitute for What the Fuck?

"I'm just sayin', it could've been completely random." Tony always saw the bright side of everything.

"Amma no tinka so! Listen, my friends, donna you let this special opportunity pass you by!" Nonna shouted back, then segued seamlessly from HSN to *The Sopranos*: "Is everyone in my life fuckin' bananas?" Using that show didn't always work, but it was amazing how often it was perfect.

As I cleared the front door, she was tying red ribbons on all the curtain rods, to keep evil spirits away at least until she could get the herbs out. I had to admit she was hardly ever wrong about people and, after all, she'd been the only one home last night, so she should know the most.

"Exactly what happened?" I asked no one in particular. Lest anyone else tell the story, Ma barreled out of the kitchen wiping her hands on her forty-year-old apron. I hadn't even had coffee yet, and already she was cooking dinner. Tomatoes spiked with red wine were simmering on the big burner, and crushed garlic was backstroking and getting a tan in olive oil in the iron skillet in front.

"Get this picture," Ma said, making a big arc with her arms. "Your father and I went to Bingo at St. Agatha's as usual, and Tony was off somewhere as usual, *not meeting* the good Italian girl he's going to woo and marry at a nice nuptial Mass and make lots of our grandchildren with." She gave her son The Look. Tony rolled his eyes.

"Nonna was here alone," Ma went on, "which didn't seem to be an issue. She was watching *Casablanca*. About 9:30, she heard the glass in the kitchen door break, and somebody reached through and turned the knob. He was wearing some sort of ski mask, like in the movies."

"*Si, si!* Round up the usual suspects! A ski mask-a. He arrived with the confidence that comes from wearing just the right accessory for the occasion!"

Nonna's *Casablanca* quotes were good, but she still had problems with QVC. Just last week Pop drove her to the supermarket, and they wound up in the fast checkout lane behind two nuns. Nonna spied the clerk with the gigantic hooters and tried a line from the Diamond Stud Earring Hour: "Every woman should have a good-size pair of these babies, and know how to use 'em!" The nuns dropped their yoghurt and it broke open all over the linoleum.

"I'll be in da car," Pop had said.

"So," Ma went on, "this character comes breaks into the house. He comes waltzing into the living room, right here, and doesn't see Nonna sitting in your father's easy chair. He starts nosing around, taking pictures off the wall. Your father says he was probably looking for a safe." Ma mimes the burglar's movements, tiptoeing from the kitchen into the dining room like Lucille Ball. "He sees Nonna's little grey head, tells her he wants some sort of pet, a cat. We don't have a cat. But we do have a Louisville Slugger up against the wall living for atmosphere on days when Tony watches baseball games, and Nonna goes for it. He goes for her. All I can say is, look for a guy with a hole in his head, casts on both arms and possibly a broken knee."

Then Nonna stepped in for the big finish.

"Amma say to him, 'So whaddaya want?', and he say to me, 'You gotta da fee-line?" Nonna didn't know what a fee-line was. And the robber didn't know what Nonna's first language was, so he tried to fake it.

"He say to me 'Felino! Felino!' It mean nothing. Then he get smart with me and say '*Gatto! Gatto!*'" That might work in Spanish, but in Italian, *gatto* has the dubious distinction of being a word that swings both ways... it could mean tomcat or pussy. This does not make Nonna a fan, as he is pointing to himself as an illustration of a tomcat. But wait, it gets better. He tells her maybe this cat could be on a table somewhere, so he asks if it's been *puttana tavola,* making back and forth sweeping motions toward the dining room. He got the table part right, but in Italian *puttana* means whore.

"*Gatto,*" he says again, pointing to himself, then "*Puttana tavola,*" he says. What Nonna got out of it, is that she's a whore and they should do it on the table.

At this point, she took him apart. Having knocked down half a bottle of *Strega* watching the "Pine Barrens" episode of *The Sopranos,* on top of the bubbly *Prosecco* she'd been pouring during *Casablanca,* she was primed for a fight.

"Amma tell-a him, '*Bastardo,* you regret it. Maybe not today. Maybe not tomorrow, but soon and for the rest o' you life... you fat fuck!'" Nonna forked her fingers and thrust them toward the street outside, in a gesture to make the bad guy's balls fall off. On the sidewalk, some innocent kid yowled and slid off his bike. Tony automatically cupped his hands over his crotch.

"I don't believe that Rick actually said 'fat fuck' in *Casablanca*," he swallowed, "but it does give new meaning to cat burglar." He straightened up and checked his pants. Satisfied that nothing was missing, he angled away from Nonna to keep it that way, and to change the subject completely.

"Not for nothin'," he said, "but guess what? I get the run of people's houses legally!"

Tony, younger than me by two years, is a cable guy and a poster child for the most entertaining kind of adult ADHD. He's also been known to sort of grease the skids for me to get inside the occasional crook's dwelling, for a little innocent information gathering. He lives at home in between girlfriend dramas. His big dream is to open an Italian seafood restaurant using Nonna's recipes, called *The Garlic Cove*. Which maybe should happen soon, since he's on probation again at work, this time for installing unsolicited TV hookups in garages where people keep their pets caged, so four-legged viewers could watch *Animal Planet*.

"Dare I wonder what you're doing home on a weekday?" I asked him.

"Took the day off. It was DEFCON 2 in here." He paused, "Plus, there's a slight possibility I could be fired, since a certain homeowner carrying a week's worth of organic waste got her sandal caught in the cable of one of those garage jacks."

I was careful not to mention a guy in a ski mask showing up in my apartment, just like at Ma and Pop's house. It would've freaked out everybody but Pop, and I had to talk with him privately. Neither of us believes in coincidence. The intruder wanted something very badly from me, and when he couldn't find it, he decided to hit my parents. He wouldn't give up now.

"Let's change the subject again," Pop said. "Vicky's on the way over, which is great. The bad news is she's bringing Sandro, which dere must be some law against, I just haven't found it yet. Nobody mentions our uninvited visitor to him, nobody asks for any help, *capice*? His version of help is six sawed-off shotguns in the driveway."

Sandro "The Eel" DiLeo is my first cousin. It's not that Pop doesn't like him, exactly. It's just that, while Sandro has aided the side of law and order from time to time - in particular, during the dicey affair that involved my former colleague Siggy - he remains the most visible "connected" member of the Santinis. He's also the snappiest dresser; and god knows outfitting his stocky, armament-heavy frame can't be easy. It's been awkward for Pop over the years, personally and professionally.

Sandro was coming over with Vicky Balducci, my best friend on this planet since day one, because they're now an item. He relocated from Belleville, New Jersey "for unstipulated business purposes", and just naturally wound up at Sunday dinners at Ma and Pop's. The relationship incubated over antipasto and cannoli, and then burst to life a couple of months ago in an eruption of spicy *pepperoncini* too hot for anybody but those two to handle.

A car screeched to a stop, and the whole family was sucked over to the windows. Sandro and Vicky emerged giggling, out of a silky platinum Lexus LS600. This was the fourth car he'd brought over in the past six months. Nobody ever asked where they came from, and he never brought it up; but every time he parked a new one, Pop wanted to go out and dust it for prints.

"Yo, Beautiful!" Sandro said to me from behind Vicky, as he ushered her up the front steps, one hand on each of her butt cheeks. "Walk single file, walk single file," he told them. He always calls me Beautiful, which makes him perceptive and intelligent in my book. And he always was good to Vicky, although her Mafia Princess look had morphed into something I couldn't quite put my finger on. Thick black eyeliner, and blonde hair so big she had to duck to walk under paddle fans.

"Where'd you get those bruises on your arms?" I asked her. "Tell me it's from the dogs." Vicky runs *Balducci's Love Your Dog* day spa. "And what's that tattoo?" It was a tiara with a bloody stiletto through it, on her right deltoid muscle. It had a "69" just below. "Or should I ask?"

"Eight hours a day clippin' canines, a girl's gotta do something else to vent her aggression. Hence, the respite of Roller Derby." Hence the respite? Sandro's mobspeak, as tragic as any dialogue in any 50's gangster film, was taking over. "They've got what they call a Fresh Meat training program for beginners. As you know, Buffalo is the Queen City. I play roller derby with the Killer Queens. My rollergirl name is Bitchin' Bitch, a reference to the dogs. I'm workin' on something a little more provocative. I'm numba 69, a personal favorite." She stifled a gurgle and looked sideways at Sandro.

"I'd try to keep that in perspective," Pop said. "Buffalo's also called the "City of No Illusions." Ma came back out of the kitchen with cookies and coffee, and the six of us settled around the dining room table.

"We have news," Vicky said shyly. Vicky is not shy, so I knew this was the run-up to something serious. Everybody stopped breathing. Nonna said what the rest of us were thinking.

"He knock-a you up?"

"Haha, not for lack of trying! No, it's this: We're gonna get married." Vicky purred the word marrrrrried. Ma crossed herself. Pop gave Ma a bewildered look and she crossed herself again. "Why not?" Vicky went on. "We'll have to do it eventually. Can you imagine what fun Christmas will be with little Sandros running around? Besides, even with Sandro's, um, resources, we could use a few wedding gifts. Bring on the envelopes!" Pop bit his knuckle in a traditional Italian plea for self-restraint.

"Wedding envelopes!" Nonna intoned knowingly, wagging her finger up and down in a *listen because I know*. "I may not be the sharpest knife in the drawer, but I have my finger on the pulse of matrimonial bliss. A wedding is the beginning of a new lifetime of sparkling dreams come true."

"Can somebody please translate?" my father wiped his forehead.

"Shhht! Shhht! Listen and learn! I'm talking about the ideal gift for every man... small enough to fit in an envelope, big enough to change a man's life."

"A condom, and that's my final answer," Tony said

"Brass knuckles," Sandro said.

"Is everybody here *nuts?*" Pop was ready to blow a gasket. He got nose to nose with Nonna and mouthed the words: "Mom... what... did... you... just... say?"

"*I* didn't say it... *Lou* said it, when he got married to Pommie. He said it to the guy who gave him the envelope."

"*What envelope?*" everybody asked in unison.

"Some suit tappa him on the shoulder and lay an envelope on 'im, a wedding present, and took off."

"What was in it?" Ma wanted to know.

"*Chi sa,* who can say." Nonna pulled down the skin under one eye. *You know what I mean.* "Nobody asks, nobody gets hurt."

Mystery envelope? My mind wandered to my nuptials. My traditional Sicilian wedding ceremony at St. Agatha of Catania was mostly for Ma and Pop. White cloth draped above the church door, a vase to be shattered after the vows, with each broken piece symbolizing a year of wedded bliss - except nobody remembered to bring the vase. The release of white doves, one of whom got knocked to the ground by flying candy-coated almonds. Santinis thrive on drama. The reception was in the St. Agatha's Bingo Hall, where Ma and her sixty-something Rat Pack conduct their social life. This Hall was the scene of Ma's infamous arrest for running her own Executive Game during penny ante poker night. Charges were dropped, but the mystique remains.

The wedding was all very cozy and ethnic, in a *Deer Hunter* sort of way. My gown was long and white, Ma's idea, since I haven't technically qualified for that since I joined Johnny Renza's fan club in school. Vicky, my Maid of Honor, along with the two bridesmaids and the flower girl, looked like cotton balls in their fluffy, ballet slipper pink dresses. We all carried roses. Mine were ivory, theirs were raspberry. After the reception, everybody headed outside. I carried my bouquet up the church steps as elegantly as I could. This was tricky, since I had as much champagne on me as in me, and my four-inch heel sandals were soggy with it, and loose. Also, it was obvious that my body had stretched a good size since the last dress fitting, and that sucking in my stomach was just throwing me off balance.

I reflected along the way up the steps on how even a borderline tubby geek like me could land a prince and be queen for a day. When I got to the top step, I handed my glass over to Vicky. I turned to face the church doors and, in a magnanimous gesture of peace and hope to everyone below, I flipped the flowers over my shoulder.

From out of nowhere, Kathy Shula vaulted up to intercept the pass. Kathy, my nemesis, the pimple on the ass of my entire existence, the last person I'd ever invite to anything, much less my nuptials, was after my bouquet.

Even in Lovejoy, it takes a lot of nerve to crash a bouquet toss. Before Kathy's long, purple acrylics could close around the ribbons on the roses, Vicky was airborne over the crowd like a badminton shuttlecock. She sacked Kathy in midair and they went down to the sidewalk, two teased blondes trading punches in a sea of pink tulle.

"Give it back, you bitch!" Vicky was spectacular. I so admired her accuracy, given the amount of *Prosecco* she had consumed. When she finally stalked away with the tattered remains of my bouquet, surrounded by admirers, Kathy was left behind spitting up concrete with a false eyelash missing, along with two acrylics.

Now, years later, Vicky had graduated to executing basically the same sort of legal mugging on roller skates. Well, good for her. I tuned back in to the conversation at the dining table; they were already going over the guest list.

"It has been my experience that men generally bring only their wives to such gatherings," Sandro was saying, "although the *goomah* has a significant role to play and on occasion is inclusive."

"You mean included," I said.

"Yeah, whatever."

"No." Vicky put her foot down, really hard. "No, just no. Listen, I'll tell you something right now, big guy, there'll be no *goomah* activity in *this* marriage. That dick of yours gets hard at the drop of a hat. If any hats happen to drop around you, old or new, you - and your dick - better be headed for the door, *capice?"* She wagged her finger in his face.

"What a woman, what a bitch," he said appreciatively. "But you're *my* bitch, know what I mean. Heh heh." His skinny goatee dipped and swayed.

Ma got up to stir the pasta sauce, and everybody helped clear the table. Alone in the living room, I tried to see the place through the eyes of a burglar. What did he want so much that he'd break into two houses and threaten me on the phone? I ran my fingers along the edge of a side table covered with framed family photos. There were no groups of relatives signing the words *The treasure is under the couch!*

I lifted my hand to open an enameled box on the shelf above, and accidentally dislodged a piece sitting behind the photos: it was Timothy Leary, the foot-tall ceramic Himalayan cat my mother loved. He had long hair, dark face and paws, and piercing blue eyes. He looked like a Siamese on LSD. He teetered for a long moment, then plunged to the floor and broke his little neck. No, no, not that! It was a symbol of family closeness, a relic of a time when I'd needed Ma and she'd been there. In the numbness of the doldrum days between Lou's death and his funeral, Ma had come over to the condo to cook for me and see her daughter through the worst. She'd always loved that cat, so I gave it to her as a thank you. I tried to balance his head back onto his voluminous body, but it wouldn't work.

From the sound of it, everybody was about to come back out of the kitchen, so I had to think fast. There were basically two options: I could be an adult and own up to breaking the cat, or I could make it disappear and live to fight another day. I went with Option B. I scooped up the pieces and sprinted out to chuck Timothy Leary's remains into the trunk of my car. It would be fine, until Ma eventually went to dust the house and noticed he was gone. This was not a daily event. She didn't even know where the *Pledge* was. Although, rumor had it she'd made it through her first five years of marriage perfecting her tan and doing her nails during the day, and then wiping off the coconut *Coppertone* and spraying Lemon *Pledge* into the air five minutes before Dad was due home. How'd your day go, Margie? Oh, you know, Dominic, the kids and the cleaning.

Ma sent me off with the rest of the cookies and of course the usual admonition, "Remember, a minute in the mouth, a lifetime on the hips." Let the guilt begin.

CHAPTER FOUR

I headed out of Lovejoy going over memories of my wedding night. After the reception, Lou and I were finally alone at the condo, exhausted, looking forward to the flight to Maui the next day. He'd been a good sport about all the Santini wedding stuff, although he did refuse to put a piece of iron in his pants pocket to ward the evil eye off his privates. What the hell, I could handle that myself. The only eyes on my husband's pants had better be mine. I went into the bedroom to change, and when I came out I was struck by the sight of him in the living room, filled with wedding wine, standing unsteadily by the fire. He looked distracted, a thousand miles away. As I waltzed into the kitchen to get more champagne, I saw there was something in his hand.

"Everything okay' honey?" I asked, not waiting for an answer. When I came back with the wine, the something was gone. It might have been the ceremonial burning of the little black book. Or, perish the thought, maybe he'd had second thoughts about that, because there was nothing in the fire. I kicked that thought out of my head, and it drifted away as we made love on the fluffy white rug. Timothy Leary sat on the floor by the fireplace, giving me a troubled look.

Back in the real world, it was noon by the time the gathering at Ma and Pop's was over, and I'd gotten back to the condo and pulled into my underground parking slot. I popped the trunk to get at Ma's cookies. It was turning into a stolen goods repository. I picked up Minsky's journal and thumbed through it. Names and dates and dollar amounts.

Probably a ledger for Cornelius's expenses, or billing for photography assignments. They were good size dollar amounts, so he certainly didn't work cheap. I stuffed it in my purse. Then there was Timothy Leary. With a steady hand and some Super Glue, I had a shot at putting him back together. The head had come off fairly cleanly; another perfectly round, one-inch hole on the bottom must have come with the cat. I was just putting them in an empty Lord & Taylor bag when something fell out. It was a plain white envelope folded in half, sort of bulky and a little bent. I could feel my life plummeting from TARFU to FUBAR, to use Daly's military-speak. From *Things Are Really Fucked Up* to *Fucked Up Beyond All Repair.*

A single word was printed in blue ink: LOU. First thought: my new husband still had a thing for another woman, and he was saving an old love letter. Second thought: it was a new love letter. *Wait until you're around people to open this, don't do it here in the garage, where you can throw yourself under the first car that comes down the ramp.* I put it in the bag with the cat and retreated upstairs.

First things first: I offloaded everything onto the couch and poured a glass of mystery red. Sometimes I buy wine just for the label, like "Cat's Pee on a Gooseberry Bush", or "Backseat Bounce" with a woman's red high heel sticking out the window of a hot pink convertible, or my personal favorite, "Bitch" in black script on a classy pale pink oval. I soak off the labels for my scrapbook, if I ever make one, and then am left with absolutely no idea what's in the bottle.

Bracing myself, I settled on the couch and picked up the envelope. If this was about another woman, I wouldn't even be able to have the meltdown I deserved in a screaming fight with Lou. I took a deep breath, sniffed the envelope for perfume, there wasn't any, unfolded it and held it to the light. The glued flap was loose and the contents fell into my hand.

It wasn't a love letter, but my heart jumped anyway because it was the one other thing a woman doesn't really want to find: a Polaroid. I turned it over. It had been taken before we were married, on a night that sticks out in my mind as the closest I'll ever get to a good-size diamond. It also happened to be the night said diamond was ripped off, in a daring and still-unsolved heist. We were there because Lou's law firm represented Ivan van Houte, a wealthy diamond importer. Van Houte had thrown a big party for international guests and influential locals, to introduce his diamond house's new collection. The star of the show was the flawless, nineteen carat emerald-cut Grey Goose. It dangled tantalizingly from 18 inches of sparkly neck chain. The rock itself was worth over six million dollars. Guests could try it on and have their picture taken and leave with a complimentary, quick-framed keepsake. I had the necklace on for about twenty seconds and never did get my picture, because some society queen apparently needed it more than I did. It was a damned free-for-all.

The particular shot in my hand was not one of those posed ones. It was candid, and was probably the photographer's lighting test. It showed Lou talking to some guy, and me chitchatting with a security guard. And the point would be what? It was a big nothing. Relief swept over me, and I got out a funnel and emptied the rest of the mystery fortification back into the bottle for later.

Next came a steamy hot shower. Which is dangerous, because it gives you space for thinking. By the time I reached for the towel I'd developed a really bad feeling about the picture. Not knowing the reason made it much worse.

I'd just dried off when Daly called. Willy Short, the gravedigger, had left a message at Iroquois Investigations. Last night Willy had been at home drinking his way through *Tarzan* reruns and, in keeping with the spirit of the thing, had elected to skip modern plumbing and go out into the backyard to relieve himself in a tall bunch of flowery white Queen Anne's Lace. All this communing with nature had inspired him to try an ape call, but he choked on it when he spied a big hole in the ground... this time with an actual body in it. He was so traumatized, he stumbled back inside the house to take it up with his pal *Evan Williams*. While they were deliberating, he passed out. In the morning, it was all gone. Everything. Grass was growing where the hole had been. "Yeah, right. And what would be the point of following up on this?" I challenged Daly. "He's plainly hallucinating." "Is he? Let's go find out." "No way." I couldn't even think about it, with that Polaroid still in my head. I did want to run it by Daly for an opinion, but I wanted to think about it first.

"I believe something's happening," he went on.

"I believe nothing's happening," I said absently. "Really, I'll bet you."

"Seriously?" Daly was not a man who took chances, and he never, ever bet unless it was a sure thing. "Okay, Janice, here it is. If you win, I'll do your laundry for a week. If I win, let's see, what could be worse than laundry. Oh yes, you'll get that Brazilian wax you chickened out of, when you were working the strip club case."

Ha, there was no way I could lose this one!

"Deal," I told him. "I'll be over in half an hour. Remember to use that nice lavender fabric softener on my jeans, and be sure to iron my cotton t-shirts, I never get around to doing that. One more thing. If you did happen to win, which you won't, how would you ever know if I actually got the wax?"

"You let me worry about that."

I rubbed enough mousse into my hair to get it under control and scrunched it into big curls, then took a long look in my closet. My hair was redder today, probably from cooking it in the hot sun at Siggy's funeral, so I decided to show it off in the clingy lime green Wolford knit dress that cost me an arm and a leg. I buy the damn stuff because I can't help myself, even though it never goes on sale; and Wolford might as well be One Size Fits All, since a size Large label represents absolutely nothing. This, I rationalize, means it's *supposed* to look like it was painted on, and therefore it's not really too tight on me. Don't laugh, it works.

With the Polaroid in my purse, I turned onto Lakeshore and headed for Daly's office on Elmwood Avenue, otherwise known as The Strip, to check out Willy Short's story.

Tango Daly put Iroquois Investigations in a plain brown wrapper on purpose. It takes up all of a two-story building that gets lost in a truckload of two-story buildings exactly like it. It doesn't even have a sign out front; but the inside is very different. While Daly prides himself on his survival skills - he could go into the jungle with a Gerber knife and a firestarter and come out with a shopping center - he doesn't conceal the fact that he enjoys luxury. His private domain is a world of rich damask drapes on creamy walls, elegantly framed paintings in subtle lighting, and burgundy carpeting so deep it snares my stilettos every time I walk in. A benefit of arriving in heels. That way, when I just happen to show up in an outfit bound to please, and Daly swings around from behind his nice, polished mahogany desk and begins undressing me with his eyes, I have to stand there and take it.

That's the downstairs. The upstairs – and I've only been there a couple of times – houses more electronics than any five men could run. And a bed with satin sheets. If a person has to spend long hours managing a covert operation from a distance, no point in doing it on the floor. There's also a refrigerator with the nutritional necessities of life, including champagne and caviar. At last count, Iroquois had fifteen door locks, three gun safes and an audio/video surveillance system. Sometimes I wonder if I could maybe order a copy of our exhilarating mind games, you know, to watch on slow nights at my apartment when Napoleon Solo doesn't show.

Oppressive heat was radiating off the sidewalk as I balanced on my black patent platform pumps with five-inch skinny heels. I hit the bell button and waved my American Express card at the camera over the door. I never use my Iroquois ID, because it wouldn't make any difference anyway, it's just a joke.

"Very funny," he said, all business over the intercom, as he buzzed me in. "You ready to go?" He was just locking the door to the upstairs. Dark silk short sleeve shirt again and drapy Italian slacks with a nice Armani break over polished lace-up shoes. Oh dear god. I took one look and got a hot flash. "Or," he said running his hand front-to-back through his short-cropped hair, which he knows makes me crazy, "we could stay here and figure out who's after you."

"Nobody's after me. He's after Ma and Pop now; but I don't see him coming back. Nonna nailed him with a bat."

"I know."

"How could you possibly. It just happened last night, and nobody called the cops." He was such a showoff.

"Nobody had to, the police are already there. Your father called. He's worried because he knows his little girl, and she didn't react to the news the way she should have. What's going on, PJ?"

"Nothing, I just didn't want them to know the same loser showed up at my place. You know how Ma and Nonna get." Nonna, in particular, adopts a retribution-first, ask-questions-later policy, and not all with a baseball bat. She knows fifteen things to do with a rosemary plant to ward off the evil eye, and only three of them are legal.

"And now there's Timothy Leary in my trunk. His neck is broken and when I went to pick up his lower half, this fell out." I handed Daly the envelope with the Polaroid.

"Timothy Leary would be...?"

"My mother's ceramic Himalayan. I gave him to her; see, he was at my condo first. There's a hole in his bottom big enough to squeeze this picture in. The only thing about it that makes it interesting is that it was taken a couple of years ago, at that party where the Grey Goose diamond was ripped off."

"I remember. The rock is still unrecovered and the case is still open, unsolved. There was an unexplained power outage, and van Houte's people weren't ready. When the lights came back, the Grey Goose was gone."

"Exactly. But what does that have to do with Lou?"

Daly was fingering the envelope, holding it up to the light, examining the way the photo had been bent to fit into the hole in the bottom of the cat.

"Your attacker possibly knew the photo was cached in the ceramic, and thought you still had it. He even said he was after a cat, at your parents' house. Before we get to the picture itself, how do you think he knew where it was?" he asked me.

"I have no idea. It's got Lou's name on it, so Lou must have put it in the cat himself. Maybe he told Ski Mask about it. But why?"

"Let's have a look." Daly strode back over to stand at his desk and lifted a magnifying glass with a heavy pewter handle out of the drawer, while I worked my stilettos loose from the carpet. He switched on his halogen lamp. "Your husband is talking to someone," he said. "Who is it?"

"Dunno, it's been years."

"That one you're talking to, he the security detail?" he asked me.

"One of them, just a rent-a-guard. Everybody else got really nervous when the lights went out, but he didn't move, I guess he wasn't supposed to. We just went back to the conversation. He was saying he wanted to be a private investigator but he couldn't pass the exam."

"He's right. His name is Kermit. I'm the one who ran the course and gave him the test." Daly taught new students periodically, partly because it was a good way to pick up operatives he'd be able to train himself. In fact, that's how he got me. "He came back and wanted to re-test, said he'd been fired. Now we know why." Daly paused and leaned on both fists. He looked at me evenly and whistled low. "So this was the big jewelry show."

"Yes, it was."

"This is why Kermit was fired. As you can see, he's making nice with you, instead of doing his job and cuffing your husband."

"Excuse me?"

"Your husband is not talking, he's taking. Look. I doubt the security cameras got it from this angle."

"He's taking what?" I snatched the magnifying glass from Daly and tilted over for a look.

In the foreground, I'm having an easy conversation with the security guard by the display case. To my right, Lou, dark-haired and impeccably dressed in a grey business suit, is leaning in to say something private to a blond version of himself. The man, clean-cut and in a blue Polo shirt, is obviously not a guest. He's holding a rolled up power cord. What's in Lou's hand is definitely not an hors d'oeuvre. You can tell by the way the giant gem catches the light as he cradles it in his palm. He is very clearly tucking the Grey Goose diamond into the side pocket of the Brooks Brothers jacket I'd gotten on sale for his birthday. Holllleeee shit! I had to steady myself on the desk.

My husband, a jewel thief? That's insane! He could barely find clean socks in his own drawer, much less pull off a world class heist. That's what the papers called it, a world class heist. The story was everywhere. When it was discovered the necklace wasn't around anybody's neck, Ivan van Houte's private security people moved in and strongarmed every warm body to submit to a pat down. I didn't mind it personally, since it was the most action I'd had all day, but I couldn't believe almost nobody else cared.

The ones who did object, and most of them were lawyers like Lou, go figure, argued they couldn't legitimately be searched if law enforcement did not officially consider them suspects. The extra-duty cop on the scene was a little hazy on the legalities of that, so a lot of folks just walked. The fact that they passed through a metal detector meant nothing, since those devices aren't designed to spot diamonds. But because van Houte's people were worried about robbery tools like knives and guns, the detector sensitivity had been turned up so high it practically picked up the fillings in my teeth. I remember I had to explain the metal hooks and eyes on my corset, and the silver Hershey's kisses dangling from my belly button ring.

"Okay, let's recap," Daly said. "Your dear departed spouse Lou has been caught on camera stealing six million dollars' worth of as-yet unrecovered income potential. And you appear to be distracting the security guard so he can accomplish that."

"But I wasn't! You know I wasn't! I didn't know anything about it! The guard – what's his name, Kermit? - was asking me about private detective courses after I told him I was a P.I. He's the one who wanted to talk!"

"One more thing: Where's the diamond?"

"How the hell would I know? Lou sure wasn't rolling in money. I went over all our financial stuff to close down his estate, and there weren't any surprises. Except that all the time we were living together, we seemed to be getting poorer instead of richer."

"You realize what this means."

"What?"

"It means he never fenced it. Maybe he got scared. Our burglar isn't after the photo, he wants the ice. He'd trade the memory card for it - and yes, these days Polaroid cameras do come with memory cards. You can bet he's ready to blackmail you – or worse – because as he said, you're in the picture too, in a very compromising position that doesn't look good. Have you heard from him again?"

"Nope, not a word." My heart was pounding. "He said 48 hours. That'd be tomorrow. And no, I have no idea where asshole Lou could have hidden it."

"I'm not saying this to scare you, Janice, but here it is: Blackmail aside, criminal charges aside, you're in real danger while he thinks you have the Grey Goose."

"So what am I supposed to do?" I croaked, and felt the hairs on my scalp raising.

Daly locked his desk and sat on the end, with one shiny dark shoe dangling lazily. He scrutinized me, eyebrows to ankles. "Stay armed. Where are you carrying your gun?" He'd warned me a million times against keeping it in my purse, or even in an ankle holster. Your purse can be taken away and your own gun can be used against you, and the ankle can be unreachable, as I'd discovered the hard way before.

"Right where you'd want me to keep it," I told him. Considering this dress was practically painted on, that left only one possibility: my thigh holster, with the weapon nestled between my legs where it wouldn't stick out.

"I don't believe you. Prove it."

"Ha, not in this life!" I made a show of tugging at the hem. "Don't worry, I've always got it under control."

"Right. Like the day the eleven-year-old got the drop on you in the movie theater."

"It was the Saturday children's matinee! Who expected a kid to pull a snub-nose out of his popcorn? I was serving a subpoena on his loser father."

"Or the night the pimp down on Planer St. took one look at your Dolly Parton wig, mistook you for one of his more successful girls, and hauled you into an alley to collect." He was warming up now, and loving it.

"That's not fair! I was having a bad hair day. I was just getting a little exercise walking to the mailbox." I started scanning the desktop for a suitable prop.

"Or, speaking of you and firearms, let's journey back to an afternoon not long ago during your latest adventure, when you were aiming for our friend Detective Longoria and instead hit the mirrored disco ball several feet above him..."

That was it. My eyes settled on the chunky black *Montblanc* Meisterstuck fountain pen stand. He saw that, and when I came up with it he deftly seized my wrist and held it. It felt like a million bucks. It always felt like a million bucks. We'd been playing at this game long enough for one of us to take it to its next logical step. If by chance we both thought that way at the same time in the heat of the moment, it could change the weather.

"Point is, big girl, keep your pistol on you and under your control. Belly band or thigh holster only, got it? Don't make me spend more time shadowing you than I already do."

"You shadow me, really?" I said, touched that he cared so much.

"Absolutely, PJ, I couldn't stand to lose you. Good operatives with big boobs are hard to find."

"Are you going to let go of my wrist?"

"Are you going to let go of the paperweight?" he said as pulled me close enough to pick up a faint whiff of his Dior *Farenheit*. Whatever is in it is so potent, it ought to be illegal. I know it's for men, but I always do a few squirts when I walk through Men's Fragrances at Lord & Taylor.

Eventually I got my breathing under control, and we called a truce... until next time.

With all the door and gun safe locks secured, we went out the back door and piled into his BMW to take a closer look at Willy Short's story. Daly is the master of the surface road shortcut, and I'm positive he delights in using unmarked streets so I have no idea where we are, which I will never admit. Fifteen minutes after we left Elmwood Avenue on Norcross, we were there. Willy's one-bedroom house was white, once, and stood on the corner of Wing Street and I'm Just Renting. Every house on the block had that absentee owner look. Nobody outside tending pansies, no names on mailboxes, no driveways without connect-the-dots oil slicks, no lawns with less than 50% dry summer weeds.

I opened the screen door and knocked on the real one until Willy opened it. Although he was in a nice, clean white t-shirt and overalls, he still had the wild-eyed look from the cemetery. Daly jumped right in.

"Why don't you show us the area in question," he said to Willy. "We'll meet you out back." We circled around and lifted the swing lock on the chain link gate to the backyard. Unlike the front, the back looked pretty good, with a small mowed lawn and plastic edging around a good-size jumble of flowers that shouted "Every perennial for itself!"

"It was right here," Willy said, standing next to the Queen Anne's Lace, pointing to a spot on the lawn that looked exactly like all the rest of the yard. "It was dug up and there was a big hole, I'd say two by four, not very deep... the guy was scrunched up in it."

"Why didn't you call the police instead of us?" I asked him.

He backed into the Queen Anne's Lace, unzipped, reached in and whipped out the tiniest dick I'd ever seen, then caught himself. "See what I mean? It's getting to me. I don't know what I'm doing. I called you because you were there when the same thing happened at the cemetery and they couldn't bury Lola. Besides, I've already called the police twice about stuff like this, and they're starting to look at me funny. First time, I was late for work and opened the garage and my car was gone. There was only a little blue tricycle where the car used to be. Honest, I'm not lyin'. I had to get a ride to the cemetery. But by the time the cops got here, the car was back and guess what, no tricycle.

"Next time I called 'em over, there was a real pig, maybe 140-150 pounds, wearing a lobster bib on my front porch, right where you were standing, tied to the screen door handle. It snuffled pig snot all over me. On that one I did go inside and knock down a couple, who wouldn't?

When I woke up I dialed 911. When they got here, wait for it, no pig. Also no lobster bib." He was fingering his dick like a prayer bead.

"Um, would you mind putting that thing away?" I asked him. "It's a little distracting."

Daly bent down to run his hand back and forth through the grass, like he was buying expensive carpet. Then, working in circular motions, he finally stopped about three feet away. He got out his pocket knife and stuck the blade down a couple of inches. With a quick flick of the wrist he popped up a corner of sod, and without much effort lifted away another two feet. By the time he was through, he'd pulled up eight square feet of brand new turf.

"This mature grass has been freshly sodded, the roots aren't even down yet," Daly said as he straightened and wiped his hands. "In a sense, it really did grow back overnight. So here's the good news, Willy, you were just drunk and somebody's having some fun with you. I doubt there was a body there, but you're really not as crazy as you look. No offense meant."

"None taken. So then," Willy turned to me, "who's trying to make me look like I'm nuts?"

"Can't say. You sure pissed somebody off. But at least now you know the truth." So that was that. For Willy's sake, I was glad Daly had straightened it out.

"I'm tellin' ya, this is too much. If I had the money, I'd get outta here. Get into a different line of work, give up the hard stuff."

"You mean go on the wagon!" I wanted to offer my full support.

"No, I mean switch from Jack to beer. Brew a whole new one. Call it *Graveyard Digger's Dream*. Folks like weird brands, don't even care what's inside."

I was about to take issue with that, then I remembered my mystery wines.

Willy disappeared into the house to celebrate his sanity and head to work, and we headed for the car.

"Oh, this is a good day, a very good day. If we hurry, we can make it," Daly said with a sly grin.

"Make what?"

"The television goddess is getting a Brazilian."

"Tomorrow."

"Today." When Daly's voice is flat like that, you know there's no point in arguing. Already Little Janice, minding her own business down where things are supposed to be secret, and prodding is supposed to be strictly for fun, was twitching in protest. *You're not going to let this happen, are you?*

"I'll drive," he said, "to make sure you don't lose your way."

When he stops at a light, let's hit the pavement!

The Brazilian wax job: (noun) The cold-blooded ripping out of the pubic hair, all of it. It is one of the most masochistic projects a woman can undertake, and it makes you look like a plucked chicken. I'm against it mostly because I have an aversion to witnessing anyone's pain, especially my own. Plus, I try to keep the number of strangers who've inspected my privates as low as possible.

"But you don't know where to go," I told him, on the off-chance I could buy some time. But he had been so sure of victory he'd programmed it into his GPS.

CHAPTER FIVE

As we drove, I considered whether this waxing would be like Carrie Bradshaw's Brazilian on *Sex and the City*. When she had hers done, the woman lifted Carrie's leg and ripped off long strips of wax, causing spasms of pain that sent her into the ozone.

All Buffed Up is a combination Brazilian wax and nail place, and lurks in a small strip mall on Corvo Street, along with a *Planet Coffee*, a tobacco shop, and an Ethiopian restaurant. Daly maneuvered a fancy U-turn into the lot and glided up to a space right in front.

"Okay, thanks for the ride," I said with just the right amount of dread in my voice. In truth, I had no intention of doing anything other than walking in the front and out the back.

I got out. He got out.

I walked to the door. He walked to the door.

I went inside. He went inside. This did not look good.

The place had two waiting rooms; the sign over one said "Brazilians" and the sign over the other said "Nails". On the upside, the clients on the "Brazilians" side looked a lot happier. My guess is it's because 99% of them were getting laid. Just a theory.

"I'll wait," he said with an engaging smile.

"Isn't that sweet," the greeter batted her eyes at Daly. She led me down the hall to a room the size of a walk-in closet decorated with a treatment table and Georgia O'Keefe prints framed in gold plastic. There's a theory O'Keefe was really painting vaginas, but she never confirmed that. The door closed, and I was left to stare at the disposable sheet in my hand... and at Daly, who had slipped in behind me. He was glued to the wall, beaming. I can't explain it, but in that moment of weakness and defeat I let him stay, setting myself up for everything that happened next.

In walked a Korean technician named Jenny, five foot nothing in purple scrubs, and all business. The three of us were stuffed into the two-person space, and already I was feeling oxygen-deprived. I arranged myself on the table and covered my bottom half with the paper. The classy Wolford dress was peeled up, and my panties went down, giving her access to the goods. She didn't bat an eye when I handed off my gun and underwear to Daly.

She went to work dipping an oversized Popsicle stick into hot wax, spreading it on one area at a time, smoothing a strip of cotton fabric over it and whipping it off in one swift, terrifying motion. The searing pain brought tears to my eyes. I bit into my knuckle and glanced at Daly, who was leaning lazily against the wall with his hands in his pockets and my black lace panties around his neck.

Jenny saw it too, and fumbled the waxy wooden stick dead center into the contested area. It landed vertical, like a battle flag, and stuck there. This only encouraged him.

"Let me assist," he said. She pretended not to hear; but she did not know Daly. He leaned over the table anyway and positioned my real estate so as to give her a better angle. I threatened to kill him and sliced into his back with my nails. When another big chunk of wax came off, I howled. He looked over his shoulder and shouted, "Push! Push!" This caused Jenny to bury her forehead in the sheets. Daly, ever the Green Beret, still would not leave it alone. He stretched out more of my landscape and suggested it had a Korean counterpart.

"Hold on, Jenny, what's this? Doesn't this look like the terrain around Pusan, or Taegu?" There was no longer any order in the room, and he was ripping off strips on his own.

"Do you understand *I WILL CUT YOUR BALLS OFF THE FIRST CHANCE I GET?*" I shrieked. Bored clients on the "Nails" side of the wall, sitting through deluxe pedicures and gel fill-ins, dropped their copies of *Hello!*

When it was finally over and I looked like a Christmas turkey, I put on my sunglasses even before my underwear to take the big walk outside. Daly pulled a twenty out of his wallet and gave it to Jenny with a wink, "Thanks for the entertainment." He paid the bill and kept the receipt. "I can't wait to see my accountant's face when I tell him to write this off."

As I eased down onto the car seat, sore Little Janice was smoking mad. *There's an old saying: if it ain't broke don't fix it!* Then I reminded her about the smiling women in the waiting room, *"There's another old saying: If you wax it, they will come."*

"I'm proud of you, Santini, that took guts," Daly said as he dropped me at my car, back at Iroquois.

"Oh yeah? You'd better hope I never get the chance to go after your privates with a roll of duct tape. Be afraid."

I had to admit it had been an adventure. I'd almost done it before, when I needed an excuse to be at a day spa during an investigation. But right in the middle, I'd taken my half-mowed lawn and hit the door.

At least, today for an entire hour I hadn't had the Grey Goose on my mind. But in the morning my 48 hours would be up and I could expect another call from Ski Mask. What should I say? I could tell him that I did have the cat, but that I threw the Polaroid into the fireplace. Then he'd say he still has the memory card, and we'd be back where we started.

Maybe I could get some ideas from police records of the diamond theft.

The cop shop I frequent is downtown, not far from my condo. The Precinct and I have a love-hate relationship. I love the information I can get out of the place, and some of the people inside - a lot of them are Pop's buddies. But I hate the feeling that one wrong step will have me at Frank Longoria's mercy. In fact, although Pop probably knows more than he lets on about the assignments I work, Daly for sure knows all about them. And if I'm ever arrested and actually get to make one phone call, it'll be to Daly. He knows I've pissed off a lot of people and he should get me out, fast. Also he'll have the media crawling all the way up Longoria's ass long before the lawyers can arrive.

At the Precinct I parked legally, for a change, and dialed my buddy Harper Frasier's cell as I locked the car. Frasier works Homicide and answers to Longoria. He also has access to the magic database that stores all the incident reports, including robberies.

"Hey, Harper, how's it hangin'?"

"Still wishin' I'd jumped on you after detention." In high school we were detention regulars, doing time for different reasons. He was punished for reading crime stories during science lectures. Me, I believed class time in general was better spent doing my nails.

"It's never too late," I told him as I walked into the building. "You can make up for it now."

"What do you need, sweet thing?" I could just picture him leaning back in his chair, feet up on the desk, well-worn shoulder holster over a crisp white shirt, lazily grazing on a wad of Double Bubble.

"A quick peek at incident reports from the Grey Goose diamond heist a couple of years ago." I wasn't sure what I was looking for, I just hoped I'd know it when I saw it.

"Oh really. I got ya. C'mon in." He shifted around as he lowered his voice. "You-know-who is out all day, having the blood cleaned off his teeth."

"That's my line. Still a classic. Be right there." I walked down the main hallway like I knew what I was doing, not making eye contact with anybody, and swung into Homicide. There was Frasier, exactly as I'd imagined him, only even cuter. He led me into a microscopic interrogation room that had been turned into a computer access area painted a cheerful shade of industrial grey. He logged on and pulled up the reports I needed.

"You've got my cell number, right? Call me if anything happens and I'll get out fast," I told him.

"Take your time." He closed the door and I watched through the window as he returned to his desk and kicked back again, as if I weren't in here violating a regulation a minute.

It was all there, all the statements the cops had taken along with the follow-up background notes. Basically, nobody saw anything. No holdup, no threats, no gunplay. I was copying it down as fast as I could. The cocktail reception had been in full swing, then the lights went down. When the lights came back up, the Goose had flown.

The Grey Goose diamond is owned by Ivan van Houte, a Dutch national. His business Van Houte & Company is headquartered in Buffalo because his wife's family lives here. He is also reputed to have personal ties in this area on the other side of the [Canadian] border.

Mr. van Houte stated he is sure the insurance company will offer a reward of at least $200,000. He stated to the people present that anyone with information leading to the arrest and conviction of the perpetrators should get in touch with BPD or Buffalo Crimestoppers.

Van Houte insists he has no enemies and knows of no personal reason for the theft. Except for possibly

The driving rhythm of my "Mission Impossible" ringtone tore into my concentration. *Now? Now, when I find out that along with blackmail, physical injury and the threat of criminal charges, there could be a reward on my head, the phone rings now?* It was Harper Frasier.

"Abort! Log off! The chief"s thirty seconds away. Sorry, babe, hurry!"

I scrambled to find the LOGOUT tab, clicked on it and prayed the screen would go dark. With one eye on the room outside and the other on my notes, I swept papers and pens into my purse. Longoria swerved out of the hallway and into the office, stopping to talk to the detective whose desk was next to Harper's. His copycat Eliot Ness hat sat on top of a mess of thick black hair that'd create an oil slick if he ever fell into the lake. The brim cast a shadow over his thin, dark mustache. The good guy hat didn't fool anybody, it just made him look as sinister as he actually was. Frasier caught my attention and imperceptibly lowered his head and his gaze. He wanted me to duck out of sight. I must have done it too fast, or maybe it was the uncanny way Longoria had of sensing danger around him, the way predators do, because he turned and looked right at me. He caught me mid-crouch, and held me there. His eyes drilled into my skull and I went icy cold.

The bastard had done this before, and I'd almost peed my pants. It was the way he flaunted his power. It put me back in the sixth grade at St. Agatha of Catania when Sister Cyril, the Mother Superior, found me and Vicky in the girls' john blowing marijuana smoke into condoms, and tying them off. Purely business. We made pretty good money with those, until Sister Cyril moved in.

But Frank Longoria was no nun – in fact, I doubted they'd even let him into a church for fear his presence would melt the statues. The screen blinked off just as he reached the door. He flung it open and the safe space between us collapsed.

"Why are you here?" Tall, dark and sociopathic, Longoria's reptile eyes never blinked. This liquidated my composure, and he knew it. I wanted to keep Frasier out of it, so I swore I'd holed up in the room all by myself.

"I was waiting for you, Detective."

"Well now," Frank's molars ground into his chewing gum like he had something personal against it, "aren't you full of surprises. Let's go." He set course for his office, and I trotted behind him. "Close it," he said as he took a seat, and I shut the door. He sized me up for a long minute, while I stood there settling on the most plausible lie.

"I'm collaborating with another reporter on a story." It was the best I could do. My plan was to elaborate on Renza's last assignment, that one corpse. Then Longoria would tell me I'd got it all wrong, I'd say I was sorry, and I'd be outta there. "I understand some bodies have been turning up in backyards around town. Are these people connected?"

"If they are, it's too late for it to do 'em any good now," he chuckled, and chewed bigger.

"I meant, are *the cases* linked?"

"Oh, are *the cases* linked," he mimicked me. "First of all, where did you hear about this?"

"Hear about what?"

"About these particular homicides."

"Homicides?" I asked, genuinely stumped. Homicides plural?

"Come on, come on, I don't have all day. This information is not public. Who told you?"

"Nobody, um, I mean nobody I can name. Can't tell you my sources, you know that."

"Oh you will, Santini, you will, and I'm already mapping out that day."

At this point, I decided the best thing to do was to shut up. He spent some time watching me sweat, then cocked his head down at papers on his desk. I shifted weight back and forth, clutching my purse to my chest, and began to hyperventilate. What a great story! There was a string of unsolved murders, and he'd told me about it himself! When he thought I'd suffered enough, he lost interest and flicked his wrist to dismiss me without bothering to look up. As I blew out of the office, Frasier gave me a thumb's up.

My heart was pounding as I sprinted to the car and speed-dialed Daly. So Willy Short wasn't nuts. And, while Daly had been right about the grass, he'd been wrong about the body. His being wrong about anything is a big deal. I was going to have a field day with this. Little Janice started twitching again. *For god's sake don't do anything stupid! It's bad enough I've been plucked naked. Next thing, he'll have me wearing glue-on sparkles and a fake mustache.*

"Daly, you were absolutely right about the grass in Willy Short's backyard being only sod. And that there was no body there. Just to show you I'm not a sore loser, no pun intended, let's run back over and have another look around while Willy's gone. Who knows what we'll find." I was in the mood to fake him out, win back my lost dignity.

"Now why would you want to do that? Did you maybe... misplace a body?"

"What do you mean?" I felt my superiority slipping.

"I mean, of course there was a body. But it was best that Willy didn't know, and I didn't want you going you out there on your hands and knees at midnight looking for more clues, digging around with a soup spoon. What changed your mind?"

"Longoria. The bastard just had his way with me, in a manner of speaking. How did *you* know?"

"The telltale finger sticking out of the ground. I couldn't believe you didn't see it."

"I wasn't looking for it, what with Willy Short and his teeny weenie within pinching distance. I'll probably be scarred for life."

"Let's keep this to ourselves, for now."

"Fine." Deflated, I hung up and headed home to try and forget the images in my head.

I knew I also should tell Renza about the multiple bodies, share the information. I thought about that all the way back to the peace and quiet of my apartment. He probably had a source he could use to develop a terrific story. If I saved it for myself, I'd be competing with him and neither of us would do it right. For my part, since my only real source, Harper Frasier, was already in Longoria's sights simply through association with me, he wouldn't be much help.

When I double-locked the door behind me and settled in for the evening, I dialed two numbers: Renza, who wasn't available so I left a "call me tomorrow" message, and Wei To Go, my favorite Chinese restaurant that delivers. General Tso's Chicken is brain food that answers all questions and explains all mysteries. With the General's help, I would sit on the new information overnight, in case an idea came to me. While I was waiting for the food, I took off my makeup even though it was only 5:30 in the evening. I told myself this would atone for all the times I'd *almost* taken off my makeup, and my skin would positively glow in the morning. I could use a little extra glow.

By 11 a.m. I hadn't come up with any new story angles, but it had been a good, solid sleep. Daisy had spent the night under my pillow, just in case. When I opened the bedroom blackout drapes, I winced as bright light poured in through the floor-to-ceiling windows. Six stories down, sailboats were bobbing in the marina; pretty soon, the early lunch crowd would be baking at outdoor tables, anticipating their *Nicoise* salads and glasses of *Beaujolais*.

I jerked the drapes closed and felt my way into the kitchen to put on some coffee. Ma, in her never-ending campaign to turn me into a classy broad, had given me an electric percolator with an etched glass carafe. A thirty-something woman apparently is supposed to know that percolated coffee tastes better, and that people who make it are demonstrating their maturity and patience. I put water in the pot and a few spoons of ground beans into the basket, efficiently placed a cup beside it, plugged it in and dragged back to bed.

Fifteen minutes later, the aroma of fresh-brewed coffee wafted into the bedroom, and it was much more pungent than I remembered. Maybe Ma was onto something. I rounded the corner into the kitchen... and struggled to understand what had just happened. Brown liquid was everywhere, but the basket and the pot were empty. It had soaked through paper towels and my shopping list, and the runoff on the counter was circling the toaster oven ominously, draining into a river that was snaking across the floor. Even the percolator top was wet. The percolator top. I'd forgotten to put it on. See, this is why it doesn't pay to get up before noon. Some of it had landed in the actual coffee cup, so I added a little Half & Half and called it a morning. I'd completely forgotten about Ski Mask when my cell phone rang and I answered it.

"Have you thought it ova?"

"Ova? Ova? Are you insane? If you're going to try to shake somebody down, at least do it in English!" I do not need this kind of aggravation in the morning.

"What're you, five?" he threw back. "Learn to improvise. Overrrr, have you thought it overrrr.?"

"Yes I have, whoever you are, and I've got a news flash for you. I know you're talking about the Grey Goose diamond. I also know four other things. One: I don't have it. Two: Your dipstick's not in the oil. Three: There's no diamond inside my mother's cat. If there were, you'd be calling me on my yacht in the Mediterranean. Four: Did I say you're nuts?"

"That was only three things, paraphrasing doesn't count. I'd give you a C-plus on that. If I were you, I'd consider my options." Somewhere between "C-plus" and "options" he started to sound dark. "It's mine fair and square," he said, "it's between me and Lou. I made it happen. Don't get in the way, it won't work out for you." I was actually beginning to understand him.

"My husband was not a jewel thief!" I wouldn't have had the guts to say that to him face to face, with Polaroid visions of sticky-fingered Lou dancing in my head, but we weren't face to face. "Anyway, why now?"

"Because, sweethot, I want my payoff. Lou died, too bad for him, at least he was getting laid."

"How dare you!" It was true that Lou checked out while we were doin' it, and I guess that kind of thing gets around. Still...

"Don't make me come back," he said flatly. "I won't be so nice about it. Your friend Mr. Daly can't always watch out for you. And you're not going to call the police. We all know how that would go." Then he took the easy way out again and hung up.

I have a problem with chills that run up my spine and betray me when I feel fear. I was literally shaking with them, now. Don't get me wrong, I'm no sissy. If I had to, I'd shoot to defend myself; but I'm a realist. He knew about Daly. It sounded like he knew about Longoria. What else did he know? For that matter, how did he even get my private cell number? I checked the locks on the front door and the locks on the sliding doors to the balcony, more as a matter of procedure than anything else. Then, in the middle of summer, I wrapped up in my big, fluffy red UltraFleece robe and curled up on the couch to think things through.

Twenty minutes later, I hadn't thought of anything at all. I needed food, preferably chocolate. But as I was already shoehorning my butt into my widest pair of jeans, I didn't trust myself to eat alone at home. Even raiding my substantial supply of Hershey's kisses in the freezer was likely at a time like this. Every dieter knows frozen chocolate tastes just as good.

So I slipped my black slacks on, a classy black stretchy tee and those nice passionate purple *Miu Miu's* Napoleon Solo had let me try on three dreams ago, the ones with the silver four-inch heels and ankle straps, and headed out.

I like to people watch while I diet – it takes my mind off what I'm not eating - so I drove around until I found a restaurant with a lot of people, and snagged the last table at a prissy white cloth place called Rentano's. I ordered the lowest calorie item on the menu - coffee - and loosened my ankle straps. In my selective memory I can't remember what month this is, but I can recall the exact second I got the sandals. They were calling my name from a boutique window on Walden, the kind of place that doesn't put the prices out front. I'm not sure how much they actually set me back, but I know I'm still paying them off at 21% interest.

I polished off the coffee in ten minutes flat, and then went for the Sautéed Mushroom Appetizer. Another ten minutes. It didn't feel like

I'd eaten anything at all. So I asked for the Bountiful Veggie Appetizer with Creamy Dip, and told the waitress to hold the dip. What's life without dip and cheese and animal fat? Tragic. She glared at me and brought the rabbit food. In ten more minutes it was gone. "Well, are ya going to order an entrée?" Her skinny bottom half was wrapped so tight in her long white apron, she looked like an enchilada, which just made me hungrier. She, along with the nine people standing around in the foyer watching me take up a table for four, wished I'd go. "Bring me the menu," I said firmly. "The big one." Celery makes me cranky. While she was gone, I stared down the mob by the door. There was one woman who was literally head and shoulders above the rest, and thin as a strand of spaghetti. I pondered the appeal of wearing pants that ride so low you'd sit right out of them if you had a normal size butt. But then, her butt was tiny, and ten inches higher than everybody else's. My eyes involuntarily traveled north of her navel, picking up a close-fitting cotton shirt hugging a six-pack that was no accident. Something about her said "Don't fuck with me." Her collar was open down to where her bra should have been. Three small hoops dangled from her left ear, through pixie cut coal black hair. Why should I be jealous? We were no different, really, we'd look exactly the same if I were stretched out a good foot and a half.

I turned my attention to the menu. I don't know how French women stay so thin, eating things like French onion soup, with all that bread and cheese. But if it works for them, who am I to argue? Miss Congeniality took the order and dumped the onion soup in front of me. While it cooled down, I toyed with the bubbling hot cheese on top, twisting it with my fork and pulling it like taffy. I decided I had to tell Renza that the body in his report wasn't the only one, according to Longoria himself, and he could do whatever he wanted to do with it as long as he never said who told him. I didn't know if I was going to tell him specifically about Willy Short's situation. Either way, the station would have a gigantic news story.

I broke my own no-cell-phones-in-restaurants rule, and dialed him up.

"So, Renza, still babysitting little Kathy? Did you take your eyes off her vibrating, feverish little body long enough to do the story on the dead one?"

"Actually, I'm working right now. Can I call you back?"

"Yeah, but this'll only take a minute, it's really important. You there? *Hello?*"

"Let me call you back," he said, and hung up.

"Damn it, damn it!" Everybody stopped eating to stare at the crazy woman's table. I dialed him back. No answer. People were watching to see what happened next.

I was at a fancy restaurant in fancy shoes, and I was not going to let this make me look bad. I breathed deeply and smiled sweetly, taking my time easing the phone facedown onto the tablecloth, so that the sparkly diamond-cut latest-thing cover caught the light. I smoothed my slacks and twisted a handful of out-of-control, summertime fuzzy hair back behind my ears until it looked like it was there on purpose. Then I stuck my fork back into the gooey cheese and concentrated on maneuvering a big, satisfying blob of it into my mouth, smiling with my eyes and lowering them as if it didn't matter at all.

On the way back up, they flew open and I about choked when I saw Renza himself blow in the front door. He did a kiss-kiss with the tall, skinny pixie-haired bitch. That being far more interesting than me, the handsome amorous reporter and the Amazon, the lunch crowd shifted attention. I wanted to crawl under the table.

I considered making a run for the bathroom, but my shoes weren't buckled on. Or I could duck under the table to work on that. But I waited too long. Before I knew it, they were headed straight for me. I was working frantically on wrenching a loose string of cheese off of my lipgloss, when our eyes met. I gave him a half grin and prepared for the worst.

He walked right past me! They settled into a corner booth, and he never looked back.

What the hell? I grabbed the phone and hit redial again. He heard it ringing and turned it off. He had to know it was me. When voice mail picked it up, I let him have it.

"You're an asshole, just so you know! The only difference between now and high school is that now you're a bigger asshole. How many women do you need at a time?" True, I hadn't technically seen him putting moves on her or Kathy on this particular day, but that's what imagination is for. And to think I almost gave him a career-blazing story. I couldn't pay the tab and get out fast enough.

Where to now? If I went to the station, Murray Soper would stick me with another story nobody else wanted. This was my second go-round here, and the rules were a little fuzzy. First time, Kathy Shula's father had been news director. I'm not sure why I resigned when I got married, I guess it was just because I could. After Lou's life insurance money ran out, I became a private detective and wound up working for Daly at Iroquois Investigations. It didn't yield enough cash, so I went begging at the station. When I was hired back, my assignment was to locate their missing reporter, Gerald Sigmund. And I did. I found Siggy - or what was left of him - and we buried him. Now I didn't exactly have a job description. Hence, the crappy assignments.

What I really needed was an outlet for my frustration, I mean besides eating. Ma would tell me to take up cooking; but why should I, when Mrs. Santini's Take Out Spot was always open? Pop would say to work another real live murder mystery; but I was, and so far all it had gotten me was frustration, more danger than I was ready for, and an excruciating pubic experience. Tony, being a cable guy, would say to lose myself in a TV show, which just wasn't my style. Daly, being Daly, wouldn't say a thing, he'd just look at me and my panties would melt. Vicky would say to kick some asses at a roller derby.

Oh really?

It was a little after 4 p.m. when I connected with Vicky. She was at work.

"*Balducci's Love Your Dog*, ya got Vicky here!" Every single time she answered the same way, and it always sounded like she was wrestling a wild animal. Sometimes there was water involved.

"Why do you skate? I mean, why do you skate in derbies?"

"That's easy. Because if I'm gonna kick somebody's ass, it shouldn't be Sandro's", she answered without hesitation.

"When's your next skate?"

"Right after work. Wanna come?"

"You bet I do. I want to see. Where is it?"

"Come over here. We'll go together. I'm leavin' at 5:30. Whatever you do, don't show up wearing TV stuff. It's not that kind of crowd."

"So what should I wear?"

"Think Kathy Shula."

"Bitch."

CHAPTER SIX

Raging Whoremoans. Hell's Angel. Multiple Scoregasm. Postal Servix. Real names of real rollergirls. Surely they couldn't be as intimidating as they sounded. I Googled "roller derby" while I waited at the rink for Vicky to change. The whole point, apparently, is for the skater called the "jammer", from either team, to score as many laps around the rink as possible on the opposing pack. They travel in packs. Naturally, the opposing team doesn't want this to happen, so there's a lot of unladylike pushing, shoving, elbowing, hitting and tripping directed at basically everybody on the other side, especially the jammer, who is easy to spot with a big star on her helmet. Sort of like putting a bullseye on a hunter's vest.

Legal places to hit include the chest, abdomen, arms, hands, hips and fronts of the thighs well above the knees. Oh, be still my foolish heart. In my mood today, I would clean up. Off-limits body parts include the head, neck, back, backs of thighs, butt and anything below mid-thigh. There's a penalty box. Bright red is a popular derbygirl hair color, so I should fit right in, even if it's only into the audience.

"Learn everything you need to know?" When I looked up, I saw a fierce looking broad, there is no other word, in a black helmet and bright red lipstick, with boobs bursting out of a hot pink, low-cut spandex tank top that said Killer Queens. Her bum was poured into matching hot pink spandex short shorts. Underneath were black fishnet stockings held up by a black garter belt. Her four-wheel skates were black, and her socks were black with hot pink vertical stripes. If Vicky hadn't already taken to wearing thick black eyeliner, I wouldn't have known her at all.

"It's me, Vicky!" she screamed in my ear.

"Holy Mother of Pearl! I can hear you! You're the one wearing the helmet!"

"Oh yeah, sorry," she shouted back, "I'm getting myself psyched up! Tonight it's the Killer Queens versus the Mayville Mayhem. They're comin' in from Chautauqua county. Last time they beat the pants off us, and our jammer got a compound fracture. It was real ugly. That will not happen tonight."

I thought she might have been exaggerating, until I saw the rest of the team. Intimidating would be too innocent a word. If any of them walked toward me on a sidewalk, I'd cross the street. Several streets. One, in particular, wasn't just wearing black eyeliner; she had smeared it around her eyes and artfully blended it into her pasty white face, to look undead. Blonde hair as straight and severe as a box of masonry nails hung down to her shoulders. It wouldn't dare do anything else.

"Who is she?" I asked Vicky.

"A real psych case. Her player name is Twisted Sister. Doesn't talk much. Anybody gets in her way, she does a lotta damage. Looks completely different in real life."

"Better or worse?" I asked.

"Hard to say."

"Awright, let's do this thing!" The official - they call him the zebra because of his striped uniform shirt - got everybody together. For the next hour-and-a-half I watched in horror as Vicky took hellacious punishment. She got an elbow hard to the solar plexus, and a fist to the wrist, but she kept on skating. This was nothing, compared to what Twisted Sister did to the other side. The woman was terrifying, partly because she was so clever she never landed in the penalty box.

Afterwards, back out at the car, doubled over in pain and with a knot the size of a walnut on her limp right wrist, Vicky insisted she could still drive.

"Feeling all better now, all rid of frustration and aggression?" I asked. I couldn't resist it.

"Yeah, actually. Look, see, there she goes," she whispered, pointing to Twisted Sister as the woman sauntered over to her taupe Ford Escape. She lifted the back hatch and tossed her equipment bag on top of a jumble of tools and clothes. She gave the emptying parking lot the once over, and took out a pack of baby wipes to get rid of the white foundation and zombie eye makeup. Something about the way she moved seemed familiar. But how could it be, I'd never seen her before. Last thing, she pulled a handful of bobbie pins out of her blonde hair, grabbed it by the crown and whipped it off.

I squinted to get a better look. Just as she turned, the lot security lights came on leaving absolutely no doubt about it. Even the shirt was the same.

It was Delia Minsky! Mousy, reserved Delia Minsky, Cornelius's hapless little sister, going to a lot of trouble to conceal her identity as a menacing, ruthless fighter. It took my breath away. I inched down in the car seat, eyes even with the dashboard. "Don't move," I whispered. "Stay absolutely still. Don't even blink."

Vicky was used to this sort of thing, hanging around with me. She'd even helped on a couple of cases. "You got it," she said through closed lips. "I just hope the light doesn't catch my hair."

In another minute, Delia had gunned the engine and was gone.

That sort of violence can take a lot out of you, even if you're only watching. By the time I got back home, the Renza humiliation was gone and I was able to hunker down for the night with a clearer head. Sprawled on the bed, staring at the ceiling, I knew I had informational pearls in the palm of my hand, I just didn't know how to string them together, and I spent the night trying.

Fact: A burglar, both here and at Ma and Pop's, had me looking over my shoulder every minute of every day and posed a physical threat. Fact: The Polaroid in the cat seemed to implicate me legally and leave me open to blackmail. Fact: my thieving husband Lou was a rat who had stolen a six million dollar jewel - I wished I could bring him back for just five minutes, to ask him what the fuck he thought he was doing. Fact: Renza didn't deserve the big backyard body news story, but was probably going to get it. Fact: There really was another body behind Willy Short's house. Fact: Frank Longoria made a big mistake in telling me more, and might now be realizing that. Fact: Both Minskys were dangerous. Twisted Sister was really Delia, a woman with a flare for showy violence and for choosing an appropriate nickname. Cornelius had been a criminal for years. My revised opinion of those two was that they deserved each other.

I wasn't trying to connect every one of the dots, that would be silly. But there was a better than average chance the bodies had some things in common... a killer, for instance. Pop and his cold case buddies, they call themselves the Ice Pack, could have something on that. The sun had been up for an hour, and probably so had the Santinis. It's never too early to call.

"Speak," Nonna answered. She got her phone etiquette from Johnny Sack on the Sopranos. I couldn't hear any more than that, because she had the living room television turned up and the dialogue was drowning her out.

"What in the world are you watching, Nonna?"

"DVD." She sounded distracted.

"I know. What DVD?"

"Shht, shht, *aspetta*...wait."

In the background, a man was intoning, "I weel glaze-a you like a donut with my deek which is as potent as *espresso*."

"Nonna! Again? Where do you get that stuff?"

"Something new, Pommie, a handsome young Italian stud also learning to speak English."

"Get Pop on the phone right now!"

She grumbled something menacing in Sicilian dialect and went to find my father. I could hear them skirmishing, Pop going for the remote and Nonna declaring her independence.

"Ama gonna getta my own TV, Sonny! Get outta here, it's a private party, go on!" An artful segue into Sonny Corleone in *The Godfather*.

Pop put the phone to his ear. I could imagine him in his thin white t-shirt, breaking a sweat over his off-the-grid mother and trying to get his breathing under control.

"Bad time to call?" I asked.

"It's like having a ninety-pound two-year-old, with an eighty-year-old brain, and a fifteen-year-old sex drive. She's even got a boyfriend, a dude with a flowin' grey beard that hasn't been combed since Buffalo Springfield was just a steamroller. He's a biker."

"Like a Schwinn biker?"

"No, like a bitchin' Lethal Black, custom-built, Baker 6-speed Harley with Blackjack wheels and a Ceriani inverted front-end kind of biker."

"Oh my god, has she been on it?"

"Not yet. I'm re-reading her health insurance right now."

"*Marrone.*" The image of my grandmother in fringed black leather on the back of some dude's bike was so disturbing it made my teeth hurt.

"Say, Pop, I just wanted to ask if there's any more from the cat burglar. Also," I might as well get right to the point, "what do you know about any unexplained bodies around town?"

"A: Nothing from the intruder. B: You didn't hear this from me, but corpses are turning up all over Buffalo. Three so far, all of 'em in residential neighborhoods. Why do you ask?"

"Make it four."

"Who?"

"Who knows."

"You call it in?" Pop wanted to know.

"Nope. I didn't actually see it, neither did Daly. He just saw a finger and..."

"Stop, don't tell me no more. So far it isn't obstructing justice not to tell Homicide about it. Of course, I get that your pal Longoria wishes you were one of them. You have a good reason for sitting on it?"

"Yep, I've gotta think some things through. Have any of them been ID'd?" I asked.

"A car mechanic. A psychologist. No apparent connection, but dere's a joke dere somewhere. They both do repair and maintenance, but I'll take a mechanic over a psychologist any day. When a mechanic screws up, you can tell it right away."

"Thanks, Pop, I'll keep that in mind."

"No problem, little girl."

"So, does the third one interest you and the Ice Pack?"

"Yep, it's been marinating a little longer than the rest, so it's harder to identify. Relying heavily on dental records, DNA. Plus, the mystery guest wasn't wearin' any clothes, so fewer leads, slower going. I'll give you a heads up when the body starts talking."

"Good enough. Catch you later, Pop."

"You got it," he said, an segued into, "Ma, come back, we gotta talk about this new thing you got goin'..."

Bodies. Break-ins. Booty. Too much, too early. I glanced over at the nightstand and had a talk with Daisy. She was frustrated too, in a Sig Sauer sort of way, and suggested we shoot up a few targets to reset our systems. After a long hot shower, forty minutes of wardrobe selection put me into my favorite Victoria's Secret red stretch cotton dress, with a sweetheart neckline and three-quarter sleeves. It was begging for black patent strappy four-inch heels. It took twenty minutes to brush out my hair, now that I'd added magnificent long extensions, a significant financial investment I'd made because Vicky said I owed it to myself to look more fabulous. Then I headed over to the range. I had to stay current and in practice, anyway.

Shotsworth Gun Range was in a quirky part of town where every business name comes with a story. It was run by Smoky Longbow. The story goes that a few years ago he inherited a cool $100,000. He cashed the check and picked up his buddy to go celebrate. To Smoky, that meant his favorite pastime of illegal target practice down by the lake. They always did it the same way: first the campfire and a half-case of brew, then the shooting. As this was in the middle of a dry summer, the campfire attracted some attention. And who should come in for a closer look, but one of Frank Longoria's homicide detectives, Buddy Telfair. He off-roads his unmarked car and finds the guys reloading.

Bottom line: shakedown.

"So," Telfair says, "I can haul you two in for this, and you'll spend the next few years making expensive phone calls to get some 12-year-old public defender's attention, from the luxuriously appointed cell you'll share with the Hell's Angels we just picked up. Or..." Telfair paused, "they don't call me fair for nothing, what's a shot worth to you?"

"To me?" Smoky said, remembering the cash in the truck. Parting with one penny of it was unthinkable. He gulped air. But he was a realist, and he knew he should make the amount irresistible, over the top. "How about five hundred?" No reaction. "Five grand?" That was a ton of money, but what choice did he have?

"Works for me. Let's do the math. My sharp ears picked up 8 rounds. Times five grand, that comes to, let's see, forty grand. Work for you?" The detective feigned genuine concern.

Smoky wet himself, a good six-pack's worth. Next thing he knew, he was $40,000 lighter. At that point, he made the wise decision to invest the rest before something else happened. He would put it into a firing range, and just naturally call it *Shotsworth*. That day he also picked up the name Smoky, when he backed his soggy pants into the campfire as he watched the detective drive away with his money. Being only five foot three, Smoky's butt was at flame-lick level.

I walked into *Shotsworth* and found Smoky behind the counter.

"Deadeye!" he said when he saw me. "How you doing?"

Deadeye. That meant Renza had been here. Renza called me that because of a little firing range misadventure I wished he'd forget.

"He still here?" I asked.

"In the back. Lane five. You just missed his shooting partner."

"Who?"

"Highrise."

"Who?"

"I don't know, but if she were a highrise, the fire truck couldn't reach the top floor."

I was working on that, when Renza came out with his shooting bag and a big smile on his face.

"So what, Johnny," Smoky asked, "just between us, is she worth the climb?"

Renza shot me a look, and I knew in an instant who she was. And he knew I knew. It was the woman from the restaurant.

"Easy, PJ, it's not what you think."

"It's *exactly* what I think. But don't mistake me for somebody who gives a shit." My blood pressure was jacked up to the red zone. "It's your life."

"I'll explain later. There's shooting, and there's shooting. This was," he made a gun with his hand, sticking out his index finger, "just regular ole shooting." Caught in the act. I'd never seen him so unsteady. It warmed my heart.

Smoky reached under the counter and produced a box of practice rounds. "As I recall it's .380, or does Daly have you carrying one of his .45's?" he said to me. " He's always got a soft spot for 'em."

" Nope, Daisy's still the one."

"Maybe I should hand this over after Johnny leaves."

"He's leaving right now," I said as I grabbed the box and a two-foot by three-foot black and white paper target that looked like a lifesize bad guy. "What lane?"

"Five," Smoky said. "All the others are taken."

I put on ear and eye protection, got to the lane and pulled Daisy out of my ankle holster. I unloaded her and put her on the small table in front of me, barrel pointing downrange. I opened the box of ammunition, loaded the practice rounds into a spare magazine that slipped into the Sig, and attached the target to the clothesline-type thingie that would move it far enough away to be a challenge.

A second before I pulled the trigger, my nose began to twitch. The scent. Lavender. No, patchouli. Here, in testosterone territory? With every sniff my nostrils flared. Yes, it was definitely perfume. This lane had been used by Renza and the Highrise. That's when my aim became sheer perfection. I wished he could see me now! Not for nothing, but an aim is an aim, and instead of going for the bad guy's head or upper left chest, I dropped six in a row into the family jewels. Deadeye, you bet your ass!

With a renewed sense of confidence, I reloaded. If I could do that, I could do the *Lethal Weapon* smiley face thing that Mel Gibson did. Unfortunately, the hot casing from the first round hurled itself not sideways onto the floor with the rest, but directly down my front, dead center into my cleavage. I was glad Renza wasn't there. Or worse yet, Daly. It's hard to look professional when you're jumping like a cheerleader with your hand down your dress.

You're not jealous of Renza, are you? I asked myself as the Toad's engine turned over in the firing range parking lot. *You're a free woman, you could have him if you wanted. Remember that powdered sugar orgy on your own dining table not that long ago, you didn't make him stop.*

I hate it when my inner bitch is right. Daly had found out about that, had seen the evidence, and it was damned embarrassing. While it was true that Daly had become the man I lusted after and depended on,

Renza still knew how to hotwire me, usually with food. I wouldn't have minded being able to ask someone for advice about that, but who?

Ma would tell me to get married again, to any nice healthy guy who would father a half dozen grandchildren. Nonna would say life's too short to be picky, as long as the guy I picked wasn't her biker. Vicky would say Sandro has five connected guys in mind, who will be over with diamond bracelets in fifteen minutes. Tony would have his hands full figuring out his own love life, the last disappointment being a sexy little kindergarten teacher who ran off with the mother - yes, mother - of one of her students during a parent-teacher conference. Pop would decline to comment, saying any answer would get him in trouble with somebody.

Because I can never leave well enough alone, I jumped from the frying pan into the fire and dialed Renza. He answered right away.

"Are we okay?" he began.

"You can only imagine," I laughed, eyeing the target I'd brought with me for a souvenir. "I feel strangely refreshed. I just wanted to make sure you weren't intimidated by my showing up to shoot." The fun with men is, they never know if you're serious.

"Me? I'm fine. Glad to see there are no hard feelings. It's only business."

"I believe I've heard that before. Didn't you say that about the organized crime sweetie Honey Summer, that stripper?"

"Are you kidding? It wasn't personal. I knew the whole time she was involved in prostitution."

"My point exactly. But I digress. I just wanted you to know that if you can keep your dick in your pants long enough to sit and talk, I have something you can use."

"You always have something I can use."

"Damn it, for once could you not get sexual? This is about a story."

"Okay, I'm all ears. Go."

I took a deep breath and decided to skip the part about how I was in Homicide looking for information about the diamond heist. "I saw Frank Longoria the other day and wound up saying something about the body in the backyard, you know, the one in your report. Only instead of 'body' I said 'bodies' and..."

"Oh, hold it, sorry PJ, I've got a call coming in that I have to take."

"No you don't! You need to listen to this! When I said bodies..."

"Really sorry, kid. I'll make it up to you, promise. Love ya, call ya."

Click.

Fine. You don't deserve this story, I'll do it myself.

The phone hadn't been back in my purse thirty seconds when Ma called.

"He's gone," she said.

"Who's gone?"

"Timothy. He's disappeared. How can a statue just vaporize?"

"No, he didn't, I have him." I started coughing and hacking, to buy some time to come up with a story. "You were busy," I wheezed, "and I needed to borrow him for, um, for a story on Italian ceramics."

"What story? I watch the news every night, and there's never been a story on Italian ceramics." Ma the detective.

"It's coming up," I lied, "part of a bigger special on Italy."

She bought it, but I knew it wouldn't last long, because Ma knows when one of her kids is lying, it's what she does. So I hurried home to put Timothy O'Leary back together.

It was disconcerting to see the cat and his head lined up beside a tube of Super Glue on the coffee table in front of the television, waiting for me to perform miracles. In the spirit of neatening it up, I shook Timothy's body to dislodge a little piece of fluffy material inside, but it was stuck. This was where a piece of kitchen equipment finally worked out. I skewered it with a fondue fork and gave it a twist. Out came a wad of toilet paper, along with some of the dried glue that had been holding it in place. Under a little gentle pressure, it felt like a big bug had crawled in and died. But it was harder, like an almond in the shell. But heavier, like... I took a deep breath and unwrapped it... like a diamond.

The diamond! The Grey Goose! Lou, you bastard, what am I supposed to do with this? I can't eat it, I can't wear it, I can't sell it! I can't even pretend I found it somewhere and turn it in to the cops, because your jackass buddy has a picture of me that wouldn't look very good in court!

The cops already wanted my hide, and so did Ski Mask, the creep with the Boston accent. They both also wanted the diamond. The only person who didn't want it was me.

I held up my American Express card outside Iroquois Investigations, and Daly buzzed me in. Somehow I made it in heels straight over to his desk at the back of his nice, comfy office and plunked the mess of toilet paper down in the middle of the fancy gold-embossed leather inlay top.

"The cat. It was in the cat."

Daly didn't ask what, he just unwrapped it.

"Well, I'll be," he whistled low. "The Grey Goose," he said, holding it up to the light.

"And my goose is cooked. Oh Tango, what do we do now?" I was breaking a sweat, and this time it wasn't because of him.

"We?" Then he saw the panic in my eyes and cut the comedy. "Easy, babe, it's okay. We'll figure this out. Where did you find it?"

I filled him in. I had to hand it to Lou, with that big blob of Super Glue on it, the diamond hadn't moved around at all and no one had guessed it was there. Then I had a brainstorm.

"I should just trade it to Ski Mask for the memory cod, er, card, and it'll all be over."

"You could, but remember there's no guarantee there isn't another copy of the picture. Or that he wouldn't blackmail you, or try to implicate you if he were caught fencing it. Or that he wouldn't try to kill you anyway, because you know too much. They're all considerations, but only possibilities. The decision is yours. "

Icy fingers slid up my spine. "Can we put this in your safe? I sure can't take it home."

"Hmm, receiving stolen property. Nobody would believe I didn't know what it was. Your friend Frank would love that. And speaking of the devil..." Daly nodded toward the split screen wall monitor that picked up images from six security cameras. At the front door, Homicide had arrived. Frank Longoria was about to ring for entry.

CHAPTER SEVEN

"What the hell?" I hissed. "How could he possibly know? He doesn't know! Quick, hide it! Throw it in the trash or something!"

The buzzer sounded three quick bursts, one would have been enough, and Daly went around his desk to hit the intercom microphone.

"Can I help you?" he asked cooly.

Longoria played along. "Good afternoon to you, Mr. Daly. My name is Chief Homicide Detective Frank Longoria, with the Buffalo Police Department, looking for one PJ Santini. She is employed here, and I see her car is here." The gum-chewing gumshoe tipped his Fedora back and stared into the camera.

"Holllleeee shit, what does he want with me? I don't know anything!"

"My dear Santini, you know so much you're a walking time bomb," he said. "Go see what he wants, but keep him outside."

We talked on the sidewalk. It didn't take sixty seconds to learn Frank had come to play a strong card. I told him to wait, and went inside to have a nervous breakdown.

"He wants a DNA sample from me," I stammered. "I need for you to be my witness."

"He what?" Daly shifted gears and squinted at the monitor. "I want to talk to him. I would keep him outside permanently, but I don't want him coming back with a warrant to have a look around. Let's get him in here. Now."

Longoria strolled in, going out of his way to look unimpressed. "Nice place you have here. Got a license for this establishment?" Daly pulled the business certificate in the black frame off the wall. Longoria waved it away without looking, as if he couldn't be bothered. Point made. He had the power.

Daly ignored it and jumped right in. "So, Detective, what's up?"

Frankie stopped chewing, put his hands in his pockets and rocked back on his heels. "Well now, your girlfriend's been sticking her nose where it doesn't belong. Again. Everywhere she turns up, when she leaves there's a body."

"Like where?" Daly asked.

"That's for me to know. So she's even been brash enough to come to my office, looking to find out how much I know about what she's been up to."

"Are you fuckin' crazy?" I wanted to tear into him. Daly grabbed my arm and shot me a *Don't be stupid*.

"And?" he said to Longoria.

"And. I want a DNA sample from Ms. Santini. Hair will do fine."

"I don't think so, Detective," Daly answered. "Unless you brought the paperwork."

"No, wait!" I jumped in and it surprised everybody. "It's no problem. How much do you want?" I asked Frank. I got scissors out of Daly's desk. "One strand? Two? Here, take three. Oh, wait, let me get you an envelope to put them in." I snipped them off and popped them into an envelope, sealed it, and wrote my name on the front. "There ya go," I handed it to Longoria.

Daly tried to stop me, but I practically forced it on the Detective.

Longoria stared at me like a glow-in-the-dark nipple had just popped up between my eyes. He stopped chewing and with his mouth half open snatched the envelope, folded it in half and headed out the door.

"Well look at that, he didn't even say goodbye," I giggled in relief.

"Have you lost it?" Daly said to me when the door had closed. "Why did you do that?"

"I didn't give him my hair."

"Yes, you did."

"No, I didn't. Instead of taking a few strands out of my own adorable head, I cut off a few from my extensions. They're imported from India and used to be attached to somebody named Amarit or Fatima or maybe Nandini, somebody said that actually means Prosecutor. He won't find his murderer with that stuff, unless he's looking in Mumbai."

Daly picked it up from there. "And Longoria is on my security video as having accepted your hair sample, donated in a gesture of willing cooperation." He gave me an appreciative glance. "I trained you well. But it's your own Scorpio craftiness in a real woman's body that makes you a force to be reckoned with."

"God, I'd love to get something on that bastard. Anything. Maybe he's playing around on his wife."

"Hard to prove that," Daly said. "He's an investigator, himself."

"He's a man. I stand by my theory that even the smartest men think with their dicks. I knew a guy who was so careful about not getting caught that he even showered at his girlfriend's house with the same soap he used at home, so he wouldn't smell different. But he was too stupid to destroy his credit card statements. One day he figured that out, and he was just firing up the household paper shredder to take care of it when he looked over his shoulder and saw his wife standing there with a glass of wine and a suitcase. 'Too late,' she said, 'the wine's for me, the suitcase is for you. See you in court.' "

Daly stared at me like he was on rolling video and somebody had hit pause. "You're my kind of woman. You'd intimidate any other man."

"Not Frank."

"Yes, even him. Didn't you see his dick shrinking? That's part of his problem with you. On the other hand," Daly sat on the edge of his desk, "for me, your ingenuity and frequent outright bitchery are aphrodisiacs."

I glanced down at the way his slacks were draping over his fine hardware and knew he wasn't lying.

"Where'd you stash the diamond while I was outside?"

He grinned and crossed his arms. "Dare to do your research on that?" His eyes were dancing, more hazel than green today, always a surprise.

I swear, it was an out of body experience, watching my hand latch onto his howitzer. What a feeling! Smooth, top quality summer-weight gabardine over a rock-hard rod so long I wanted to measure it and Tweet. Only, this twit doesn't Tweet. Not since I typed out a fantasy post, "Kathy Shula, the girl with the zipper tits", and my phone went ahead and posted it. She'd had them bumped up two sizes, A to C, one winter when she was "out sick". Mine are natural DD's, to go with my wide wheelbase XL hips. It all evens out.

Now, Daly was tracing my cleavage with the tips of his fingers.

"What's this?" He'd found the red mark the hot bullet casing had left. "Looks like a burn. You and Renza switch from the dining room to the kitchen?"

"There's no Renza."

"Good. You deserve better."

"Oh yeah?"

"Yeah. You deserve me, and you know it..."

"He said humbly."

"Humility was never my strong suit." He was right about that, and I liked his nerve. Suddenly, I wanted nothing more than to be in his arms. What was it that I needed the most? Protection? Drama? Sex? I'd work that out later.

"Show me the upstairs again, Tango. I need you." The immediate threat had passed, but I felt a terrible brooding sense of danger. Something more was about to go wrong.

He unlocked the door to the stairs, and this time I led the way.

"This could get complicated," I said over my shoulder.

"You mean, don't shit where you eat? You should know by now that priorities have changed. Us first, work second. That's what makes us so good."

"That's what makes us so dangerous. There's the laundry room."

"What laundry room?"

"The one in my head."

"Is this a girl thing?"

"It's always a girl thing."

"You're the kind of challenge a woman should be. We think alike. Sometimes being with you is like being with a guy. You're me, with breasts." He ran his finger down the middle of my back, so slowly it sent electricity around my waist. And then down the center of my butt. "Magnificent breasts made for sex, and for babies."

"Oh yeah?" As we climbed ever so slowly, I created an analogy he could understand. "Well, guy to guy, lay off the baby talk before I lose my hard-on."

And then we had arrived. There. Together. Alone. Along with all the fancy technical investigative hardware, the second floor contains provisions and comfortable, but cramped, living arrangements for Tango Daly and as many as three other people. This means three fold-out cots and one fabulous double bed, since Daly uses it most of all, working cases that require twenty-four hour vigilance.

I threw myself down on the low bed in what I hoped he'd see as an irresistibly sensual move, praying my red lace garters wouldn't pop off the stockings. I tried another catalog pose, sinking into the thick foam mattress topper and really silky sheets. By now, my Italian butt was about a foot off the ground.

He headed for the wine cooler and took his time. "You say you need me." His practiced hands coaxed the cork out of a bottle of *Veuve Clicquot*. It gave in with a sigh, just as it should.

"Yes, I do." I hoped honesty didn't make me sound weak.

"Here's what I need." He poured into a sparkling, crystal champagne glass. "I need to empty myself into you. I need to possess you, to take you. Not just that." He filled a glass for himself, and stared into it. "I need, I want, us to meet in the middle. To pour ourselves into each other. I love you, PJ."

I couldn't even blink. He was serious. I was serious. One did not take this lying down. So I got up. Well, part of the way up. Strappy four-inch heels don't find the floor by themselves. Newborn calves who have never stood before have done it better. Tango put his strong arm around my waist and lifted me the rest of the way.

"You don't have to answer right away. At least, not to the last part. The first part, however, is fully urgent." His eyes smiled into mine. Of all his looks, I had never seen that one before. He had never let me see it, because it was so telling. And all that time, I'd thought I was the only one who was afraid of showing too much.

His lips parted. My brain melted. By the time the fever reached Little Janice, she was twitching for joy. *See, now, this is a reason for a Brazilian! Right here, you're looking at a guy who's already seen it and isn't grossed out because of this Christmas turkey look. Jump on it!*

I could feel my nose beginning to sweat. Tango offered to help me out of my dress, and was blown away by my red corset.

"Leave it on," he said to my girls. "We can turn you loose later."

Watching him shed his clothes, I was only a little nervous. Mostly, I was fascinated at how he looked exactly the same, just without them. Like when you lift clothes off of a cutout doll. In real life, most people look different. I think. The only thing I knew for sure was, oh happy day, that you could write the entire Preamble to the Constitution on his dick. If this had been a different situation, I would have asked how he could possibly walk.

Time stopped as we stood looking at each other. First his gaze held me, then his arms, as he lowered me onto the bed. His kisses were, how can I say it, strategic. He kissed my lips, and kissed them well, until he had taken them. With his mouth on my neck, our bodies were tangled together, legs wrapped around legs, generating enough heat to confuse the smoke detector. Our hands never left each other's bodies.

I'm not exactly sure how he undid my corset, or when. Mental note: ask exactly how he developed that talent. But not now. Maybe he was right about my breasts. He spent a lot of time winning them over, so that when his mouth left, they yearned for him to come back. With Tango, they would never crave attention. I was sucking on my own fingers when I realized he was south of my navel.

"Oh Janice, my god." I could see only his eyes, and he looked really worried. "I just realized I forgot the cranberry sauce and sweet potatoes."

"Damn it, I knew it! Getting plucked wasn't my idea!" I went for his head, but he pinned down my wrists and started doing the alphabet with his tongue. Cursif is definitely underrated. When he got to K, I went out of my mind. By S, I was begging him to stop. By Y, I was begging him not to.

And then he filled me with everything he had promised, and we did meet in the middle. We met until neither of us could move.

Everything was so natural, as if we'd been making love all our lives, as if everything we had done had been for this. At least, that's the way it felt to me. The laundry room was drifting further and further away, and seemed less and less important. *Be careful, he's a man, he can't help it. When he calms down and starts thinking above the neck again, you'll be the only one making promises.*

That was when I realized he was still covering me with his warm, sturdy body. And I felt safe. As if he'd read my mind, he made a simple promise. "You will always be protected this way."

We lay in the afterglow for a long time. Slowly, the real world began to return. I did feel much more relaxed. I could think better. At least professionally. I'd been trying to be way too logical. Idly licking one of his fingers, I made a decision. Give up the diamond. Just give it up, no strings attached. If the Grey Goose were out of my life, Ski Mask would be, too. Hanging on to it was not insurance that he wouldn't use the memory card anyway, if he even had it. Technically, I could wake up tomorrow and see the picture on the front page of the New York Times. Or, he could even slip it to Longoria. Maybe he already had. Maybe that was why Longoria had asked for a DNA sample. I was just exhausted from the pressure and wanted a clean way out.

Daly, who was close to ID'ing the guy, wasn't inclined to agree; but his inclination changed when I gave it a little more lip service. "Mmmm Tango, please help me end this my way...."

It took some time to get a very sore but smiling Little Janice onto the car seat and buckled up. I didn't know how Tango and I would handle our feelings about each other, but we agreed we'd try to keep personal and professional separated.

At least I knew the diamond was someplace safe. Daly had secured it and still hadn't told me where, so I could honestly say I didn't have it and didn't know. But this mess wasn't his to clean up. Little Janice, who hadn't wanted to leave him upstairs, agreed. *You let him talk us into a Brazilian, and he makes it worth our while. But now it's up to you to get us out of this. Think!*

I went home to do that. But the truth was, I was happy and satisfied and in love with a hot man I admired, who loved me back, and I didn't give a damn about anything else at all, the entire night. And I deserved it.

WHEN I WOKE UP JUST before noon, my mind was ready to roll. I realized Delia Minsky was a bigger problem than she seemed. So good at subterfuge, so ready to cause pain. I wondered what else she was up to. If I could hang out in her neighborhood, I could watch her house. Of course, I'd need an excuse to be there, like walking a dog. Like the dog I was going to "borrow" from Vicky's business. I speed-dialed her.

"*Balducci's Love Your Dog*, ya got Vicky here!" I could hear a fire truck going by, and one of the dogs howling at it.

"Hey girl, who's the *mezzo-soprano*?"

"It's Oliver. Aren't you a good boy, such a gooood boy," she cooed, scratching him under the chin. "I know what you're thinking, and yes I do scratch Sandro exactly the same, just in a different..."

"Yeah okay, that'd be too much information, for both the dog and me. Listen, I need to borrow one of your boarders."

"What's up?"

"I'm going to stake out ole Delia, your favorite freaky derby girl."

"But she knows you!"

"Not with the wig I've got, you know, the long brown one, and the horn rim glasses."

"Gonna use the hardhat and the clipboard, too?"

"Nope. They were in Sweet Boy's trunk when he was ripped off, and there's no point in replacing them." I still had every intention of getting my Mercedes back, trunk contents and all. I just hadn't figured out how.

"Well," Vicky whispered, "it happens that by sheer coincidence I've got this Weimaraner, Oliver, while his humans are on a Canadian cruise. They just dropped him off. What a nose he's got!"

"And vocal range. How long's he in for?" I might need the same dog for several days.

"At least two weeks. Can I come too?"

"If you behave yourself. When can I pick him up?"

"Lunchtime."

I took a shortcut from Iroquois Investigations, down Shelton to Jacks and arrived at the pet spa just as Vicky was drying off a big, skinny, shorthaired, short-tailed taupe creature, on a soaking wet purple mat beside a big aluminum sink. He flapped his long, smooth ears furiously, almost knocking himself off his feet, and got her right in the chops.

"Yech! PJ, meet Oliver. Ollie, meet PJ." He blinked and gave me a deadpan Buster Keaton look that said, "So, what now?"

"Some things you need to know about Weimaraners," she said as she carefully avoided toweling off the dog's privates. "I dunno, I just can't get into that. Anyway, they're smarter than most humans I know. They think they really are human. The difference is, when they're devious they don't know they're being naughty.

"And he'll stick to you like glue. They're called Velcro Dogs. Your days of making a trip to the toilet by yourself are over. And here's the part that might come in handy in your line of work. Over half their brain is devoted to the sense of smell. They're part bloodhound. Don't even think about hiding from him, he'll find you. He's also very protective, and all muscle, bred to hunt big game, like bears."

"What do I feed him?"

"Whoever you want."

Just talking about food made me hungry. When I suggested eating, Vicky never fought me on that. "Perfect! We can go to that place by the park. We can leave him in the car in the shade, with all the windows rolled down. He's trained, and he'll stay."

We drove the Toad to let Oliver get used to it, and parked under a big tree across from Souper Salad. It's a little place open only for mid-day business, with six tables and tons of takeout. It's run by two hippie women who haven't shaved their legs since Janice Joplin rolled her first joint, and who serve whatever they damn well feel like that day, as long as it has lettuce or it fills a good-size crockery bowl. You pick up a polished apple from a big basket on the way out.

We got lucky and found table space. Let me rephrase that: two girls who were dallying over their Cokes looked up and saw Vicky Mafia Princess eyeing their seats, and split. We scooted onto the long bench against the wall beside the open door, in our jeans and sneakers, and almost blended in. The Cream of Broccoli soup was hot and fragrant, and the Caesar Salad was delicious and cold. We dug in and launched into recaps of our lives.

"The hills are alive!" I told her. That's from the Sound of Music, and code for "I just got laid."

"Really? Who?"

"Thanks a lot. What am I, a slut?"

"A woman's gotta do what a woman's gotta do. Let's see, S-L-U-T. Santini Lovin' Under Tango, am I right?"

"Right. Right!" I couldn't stop smiling.

"How about you?" I asked. "How's the wedding ceremony coming? Gonna strap skates on Sandro?"

"Yeah, that'll be the day. Don't get me started. My dress is easy, you and I can cover it in a day, with six bottles of champagne and two straws. His jacket is the issue. He doesn't want plain black, he wants *shiny*, like black ice. How warm and cozy. But..." She stopped.

"What's wrong? What is it?"

"Don't look now," she said real low, "but for the past ten minutes a certain somebody has been sittin' next to you on the other side."

"Who?" I whispered.

"Dunno, maybe some new boyfriend."

I let my eyes lead the way, twisting slowly toward the door, and we came face to face. It was Oliver, sitting on the edge of the bench with a little thought bubble over his head, "What, you got a problem with this?"

"Like I said," Vicky picked it up, "they don't know they're dogs. Wait'll you see him counter surf in the kitchen. Your refrigerator has a big handle, too, and his info sheet says he can open it. His personal favorites are turkey pastrami and Jarlsburg cheese."

"Well, at least the dog has good taste," I said, eyeing Oliver with new appreciation.

It was a particularly hot Buffalo summer, as the barometer dropped through the floor and storms prowled Lake Erie. If a person didn't have to be bothered with earning a living, this would be an afternoon for a siesta. Once I'd dropped Vicky back at work, I had a choice: I could be responsible and go to the station, where I'd get stuck with some menial, feel-good story like the one before last, the "Purrfect Pussy Dress-Up Contest". I was the laughing stock of the 6 o'clock news. We got letters: "Did PJ dress hers up, too?" And an envelope filled with pink marabou: "See if this works." They were almost as humiliating as the ones that came after I got to co-anchor one time with a guy named Dick Burns. A viewer sent a big jar of Vaseline with a note scribbled in crayon, "I hear you're anchoring with Dick Burns. Here's something that'll ease the pain."

So, today I had a choice: I could run by the station or keep driving. Driving out to Delia Minsky's neighborhood, with the potential for something way more interesting. Technically I'd still be working on a story, I just didn't know what it was.

I threw the car into gear. It lurched forward, sending Oliver into the back seat. Our eyes met in the rearview mirror, and we understood each other perfectly. He shot me a *You need me, so don't fuck with me.* I reached back to give him a chin rub, and he flapped his ears and lay down with a satisfied grunt. *That's better.*

We zigzagged through empty backstreets and finally arrived on Macduff Lane, down the block from the Minskys' cute little place that was primed to be jettisoned into the next generation, if Cornelius was at home with his O^2 and still smoking. Her Ford Escape was idling in the driveway. Up on the doorstep, Delia - she was back to looking unremarkable - was helping Cornelius make his way toward the car. His portable oxygen tank was in a carrier slung over her shoulder. When he'd settled in and she'd stretched the seatbelt over his giant frame, he flipped her off... which in their family apparently means "Thank you very much, I appreciate the effort, especially since I am an obnoxious, ungrateful moron and you do this for me anyway because we share chromosomes."

Complicated and confusing, the Minskys were an interesting study in sibling rivalry. Oh hell, they were a freak show. All questions, no answers. Call me crazy, but the woman's personality - split right down the middle - was every bit as menacing as Longoria's. His vibrations were cold and methodical, while hers were fiery and unpredictable. Both were unsafe.

Lost in trying to sort through that, I had only seconds to duck out of sight when they blew by. I'd planned to stop farther away and put on my wig and glasses and walk the dog, but now, what for? They were gone. Nobody was home. The Toad burned up five dollars worth of unleaded, while I considered my options. Was it really Breaking and Entering if a person were simply going back for something she'd forgotten inside? I could've left lots of things, a lipstick, my pen, my sanity.

No telling how many neighbors would notice if I just looked friendly and walked in like I knew what I was doing, and no telling how many would call the cops. Their row of houses on Macduff backed up to an alley wide enough for a garbage truck to get through. I circled around and parked behind number 24.

CHAPTER EIGHT

Oliver was snoozing. I left the car running with the A/C on, got out and quietly pushed the driver's side almost closed, for a quick getaway, and marked the time on my watch. I'd allow myself three minutes. Delia's Certified Wildlife Habitat sign was prominently displayed beside the back walk, as it wound through an unruly mass of flowering perennials. They'd left the kitchen door and screen door unlocked. In case anyone was watching, I pretended to knock and then put on a decent show of leaning in and silently yoohoo-ing to ask permission to go inside.

The kitchen looked exactly as it had looked when Delia showed me through. She and her brother must have inherited it from their parents. The floor wore the original layer of 1950's green linoleum, in pretty good shape, and the vintage curvy chrome-and-vinyl dinette set sat in a pool of afternoon sun, with a centerpiece pot of marigolds soaking up rays. No surprises, and nothing very personal lying around, presumably because the house was on the market. It was inviting and uncomplicated. Yet something didn't fit. It looked too clean to smell the way it did, faintly sweet, subtly metallic. Sixty seconds gone. I turned my attention to the living room and swung around the corner to have a look.

The scream that swelled in my head nearly blew it off, and my eyes bugged out a good inch. Nobody else heard it, because somebody had clamped a rough, hot hand over my mouth. In front of us, wedged into the overstuffed chair in the corner, sat Cornelius. In his hand, a cigar was burning down fast. He looked surprised to see us, but more surprised at the bullet hole through his heart. The red was spreading fast. The smell was fresh blood.

"Janice, it's me. Don't scream." It was Johnny Renza behind me. His voice was firmer than I'd ever heard it. "Do you understand?" I nodded yes, and he loosened his grip. This was a side of him I'd never seen before, and I couldn't help making mental notes for review later over a martini.

"What are you doing here, are you insane?" I wheezed. My blood pressure was through the roof. "Do you want to get us killed?" I had no idea exactly how that would happen, but I hate not calling the shots and it seemed like a good way to put him on the defensive. "How long have you been here?" I asked him.

"Just before you. Got a call. I came in the front."

"I came in the back." Which he knew. Time stood still as I scanned the room for gunmen, weapons, more victims, anything else we ought to know. I pointed stupidly at the body. "If this is Cornelius, who's the guy who just left with Delia? I've been trying to explain to you..."

"You'll have to fill me in later," Renza interrupted, peering out the picture window. "We've got company." Delia was about to pull back into the drive already. She was minus her passenger, and the garage door chain mechanism had gone to work. But I had to postpone my heart attack, because of the clatter of chairs in the kitchen. We turned to see Oliver skidding across the linoleum and onto the polished hardwood living room floor, backpedaling till he hit the coffee table. When he finally pulled himself to his feet, he did an ear flap and lifted his snout.

"Owoooo!" he howled at the scent of blood. Then he spied the source of it, Cornelius. Their eyes locked. Oliver's tail went stiffly horizontal and his head went low, making an arrow-straight, nose-to-tail line. A front paw froze mid-step. He was pointing. Stalking. Facing off. Determined not to blink first. But Cornelius had the drop on him, there.

The sound of Delia's car engine had muffled; she was rolling into the garage. Every molecule of the dog was focused on Cornelius, as he inched stealthily toward the chair. It did occur to me that startling a large, muscular hunting animal by tugging at his collar was not the smartest thing to do, but it was the only thing to do. "No, Ollie, no!" It broke his concentration. Any moment, Delia would appear. Her car door hadn't slammed yet, so we had maybe thirty seconds. Then Oliver pulled away and made a final lunge at Cornelius's free hand, jerking it left, right, violently and rhythmically with his strong neck. The corpse came loose from the big chair and listed toward the dog, leaning down with the momentum as if to pet him. This freaked out all three of us.

As Pop would say, it was all assholes and elbows as we bolted out the back. Renza went left, sprinting down the alley, and Oliver and I hit the gas in the opposite direction. I looked over my shoulder in time to see Delia surveying her property at the opening screen door, through narrowed eyes and set jaw. Assuming she had not seen us would be a big mistake.

For the next half hour, I let traffic take me wherever it wanted, trying to shake the pictures in my head; Cornelius had looked bad enough when he was alive. Obviously his sister knew he was dead, she'd killed him herself. But why? She was so close to moving out and starting her life fresh, just Delia and her schizoid, rollerskating other half. Maybe her brother didn't see it that way. In the shape he was in, he would have needed to have somebody around to take care of him, and who else could it be, who else would put up with him?

This was clearly a time to invoke Pop's secure data mining process, Dominic Santini's "Nonspecific Information Exchange". I knew he was plugged into what the police department was doing, and he knew I craved details. While he usually wouldn't just offer me information, we could sort of feel each other out. I dialed his Cold Case office in the basement.

"So Pop, anything new?"

"Always."

"I mean, anything new in the past couple of hours? Or any reports of somebody getting a jump on hunting season?"

"Aw geez, Pommie, you're givin' me ulcers. Tell me you didn't find another body."

"If I tell you that, will it make you feel any better?

"Only if it's the truth."

Long pause.

"So, Pop, some weather we're having," I said, changing the subject. It told him everything, without specifics.

"Really." He pondered for a moment. His little girl had found a fresh one. "Nope, nothin' new. You taking care of yourself?"

"Yep, I'm fine."

"You want to come spend the night over here? Your Ma's fixin' her Eggplant Parm, just the way you like it."

I said I had some things to do. We'd actually told each other quite a lot. He'd said there was nothing new, which meant Homicide didn't know yet about Cornelius. And nobody had reported shots fired. I didn't deny finding a body so he knew that, in fact, I had.

When I got off the phone, I took Oliver back to Vicky for some TLC, and probably doggie Valiums; what a story he had to tell the others. She said I could pick him up any time I needed him, that he didn't mind life in the fast lane with a crazy woman. I drove around some more, then realized that out of habit, or maybe out of fright, the Toad had brought me just down the street from Iroquois Investigations. I'd come to think of it - and of its owner - as my safe place. I walked in unsteadily, which told Daly a lot, since I pride myself on being one with my heels, regardless of circumstances. *Give yourself some credit, Santini, you're a tough broad.* Yeah, not that tough.

"You okay?" he asked. "What's going on?" I plopped down onto his nice, comfortable couch and sank deep into the cushions. He settled in beside me, propping an ankle up on one knee, with his arms stretched out across the back. Lightweight cashmere-blend dress socks, probably Italian, I'd know them anywhere. The Saks Off 5th Outlet Store is my third home, DSW being the second.

"I was just over at the house of a crazy woman, Delia Minsky."

"By invitation?"

"No."

"Go ahead."

"I met her doing a story on the economy. She's also on my friend Vicky's roller derby team. A real head case." I filled him in on all of it, leaving out the part about how Renza had sort of turned me on over at Delia's place, acting so decisively and all. "So it turns out the sour Cornelius did have a heart, because somebody took a clean shot at it. Looks like it was his own sister."

"He was a photographer," Daly said.

"Right."

"I did some research. Your husband's law firm hired a company by the name of C.M. Photography exclusively, for all events."

"Yeah, so?" My underwear was getting tight again.

Daly leaned back and waited for me to process it. "You're going to love it," he grinned. It took some time. Then it hit me like a frying pan to the face.

"Oh my god! C.M. is Cornelius Minsky! Lou's company hosted the reception for Ivan van Houte, for the Grey Goose diamond, Cornelius was shooting the Polaroids. Cornelius caught Lou with the diamond!"

"Right. And I'd say the guy Lou's talking to so casually while he's clearly pocketing the goods is the photographer's assistant. Which means they more than knew each other. Which means we're looking at Ski Mask. Your erstwhile concierge, Javier, described him as blond and around five foot eleven, about the same as your husband."

"Oh my god! This makes him very powerful and very dangerous. But who is he, really?"

"Came through ten minutes ago. He's Steuben Neely. Nickname is Wristshot. We can only pray it has something to do with hockey."

"Oh happy day! Where does he live? Can I mail him the diamond?" At this point I'd actually do that. Then I could concentrate on the bodies.

"Not so fast." Daly turned toward me, and we were nose to nose on the couch. "Upstairs, toward the end of our conference, you put extra effort into explaining the importance of ending the Grey Goose-chase your way. Such talented communication gets a man's attention."

I didn't want him to know that the pleasure was all mine, so I rolled my eyes.

"Our investigator pal, Rick, has been carrying around a picture of Neely, on the off-chance he might spot him on the street. And guess what, he's sure he saw him at his gym. The guy was switching out his shoes, getting his things together to go, and Rick was just coming out of the shower. He couldn't follow him, but he does remember something important: Neely didn't lock his up gear. No lock on the locker equals easy access. Ole Wristshot could have some trouble getting his street shoes back on next time, with a six million dollar rock in the toe."

"But when..."

"We have to wait for him to come back. I'll let you know."

"God, I can't wait, I can't wait, I can't wait! Yes! Thank you!" I threw my arms around him, and caught a tantalizing whiff of Break Free gun oil and Fahrenheit cologne. See, that'd never work for a woman.

"You're welcome in advance," he said to my lips.

With Wristshot Neely all but out of my life, there was no time to lose in getting the goods on Delia, and saving myself in the process. This required borrowing some things from Daly, specifically night vision things.

Delia had done a clever job of getting an actor who looked like her brother to appear to be leaving the house voluntarily, right down to the very public middle finger salute. But she was going to have to get rid of the body soon, probably after dark. I'd be down at the end of her street, in practical running shoes, hunkered in the Toad at a right angle to her house in a vacant lot with plenty of other cars, waiting for her to make her move. It could take hours.

And it did. Fortunately, there were enough *Hostess HoHo's* in the backseat to see me through.

By 11:30 p.m. the last of the sugar high had worn off and I was fantasizing about sleeping in soft, 400-count sheets in my own bed, when her garage door went up and light flooded the driveway. Delia guided her SUV past me. Before I could hit the ignition switch, Daly's car slid alongside and the window rolled down.

"Get in," he said. "Bring the gear."

I hustled into his BMW. "What am I going to do with you, Janice? You didn't even notice I was parked two cars away. This is not a job for one person, or even two. I've got Rick falling in behind us." Rick was one of Daly's favorite operatives because, like Daly, he'd been Special Forces and was pretty much ready for anything. In fact, also like Daly, he was disappointed when nothing went wrong. "He's in his grey Plymouth."

"That rusted out old thing?"

"That rusted out old thing is a Road Runner with a 440 engine. Now you see it, now you don't."

As he was right. I shut up.

Delia turned right on Scotland and followed it all the way to Lawrence. We had to duck behind a gas station when she stopped to run into a convenience store. She came out carrying a white jug, what looked like a quart of milk.

"Bleach," Daly decided. "She's got work to do on blood stains. Not an amateur."

Delia continued along Lawrence for a couple more miles on streets that were deserted, making it harder to follow without being seen. At a four-way stop, she hung a left into a small subdivision, and eventually drove to a brick ranch-style house at 139 Hammersmith. She turned at the driveway and pulled all the way in, looking right at home as yet another closing garage door became her curtain of secrecy.

"Gun?" Daly asked, and I nodded yes. "Radio?" Check.

We like to use radios instead of cell phones. Although not as private, they're less complicated and harder to trace. My incoming sound came through an earpiece specifically molded to my own ear, called an IFB. I always use the same one I wore on television, when the producer in the control room talked to me during a live broadcast. Whether I'm out reporting on the street or sitting on the set in the studio, it's my personal electronic umbilical cord.

Daly got hold of Rick. Rick would cover the front of the house, in case Delia decided to leave fast. There were no alleys, so with backyards butted up against each other she'd be using the street. Daly drove us around to the next street, in hopes of getting a good view of her backyard. He would run the operation from there, parked in shadow, in a cockpit with so many readouts and dials it looked like air traffic control. I'd go on foot with night vision equipment and a long camera lens to document whatever I could. Of course, that'd mean inviting myself onto somebody else's property, but I'd already decided I was going to say I was looking for my cat. Named Homer. With one eye. Wearing a red collar. With a bell on it. I'd gone over it so many times, I was starting to believe it myself.

I pulled the wig-du-jour out of my purse. In no time at all, I'd bobby pinned my long red locks against my scalp, and had a wig of chin-length, straight brown hair stretched down around my ears. The straight-cut bangs covered all the strays in the front.

"Julia Roberts, eat your heart out. Now who's the 'Pretty Woman,'" I murmured, and popped a piece of gum into my mouth.

"How much for an hour?" Daly asked.

"You can't afford me."

"You know, there are are times when I think that, myself," he said, "but not because of money."

I let that one go, since I have my own issues about commitment, and manufactured a slow, provocative hooker's wink.

"Something wrong with your eye?"

"Smartass."

There were no bobby pins left over to secure the wig to my head, but it was on so tight I didn't see a problem. I wasn't going to be doing summersault sex in it.

The night was hot and damp, and low clouds were drifting over the sliver of a moon. The house behind the 139 Hammersmith target had no exterior lights on, and none on in the house; everybody must have gone to bed. I slipped into their front yard and then, hugging the shrubbery as much for guidance as for cover, felt my way to the rear. Crouching low against the back fence, I propped my Canon digital camera on it. The night vision apparatus and the long lens made it too heavy to hold steady without resting it on something. I waited. And waited. Bent into a half-sitting position, my thighs were screaming for help, and I vowed to hit the elliptical machine hard to beef up my muscle tone if I got out of this in one piece. I had a really bad feeling about that.

Ten minutes went by. Twelve. Twenty. Twenty three. Now my calves were cramping and I did weight shifts to stretch them out, nervous that the camera lens would bob up and down in the available light, telegraphing to Delia that someone was there. Even on a night like this, the glass will show if the angle is just right. At twenty five minutes, the kitchen lights of 139 Hammersmith went on briefly and then off, as if she'd been looking for something and had killed the light when she found it. The back door opened and Delia showed herself. She was wearing a pair of long, yellow dishwashing gloves and carrying a good size butcher knife. She knelt in the grass beside the flower bed and went to work on the sod with surgical precision. In only a couple of minutes, she'd managed to carve out and pull back a huge piece, several feet square.

"She's taking out a big piece of sod," I whispered into Daly's radio, "but it doesn't look like she's going to bury him, because she didn't bring a shovel. Plus, for a guy Cornelius's size..."

"I know, you'd need heavy equipment. Very funny. Anybody else?"

"Nope. I'm shooting pictures anyway, because she's definitely up to something. If she's not putting something in the ground, maybe she's fishing something out. And..." I steadied myself and got ready to shoot.

Suddenly Delia stopped moving and straightened, cocking her head to listen to the night. She scanned without moving her head, and the whites of her eyes flashed as they caught the low level ambient light. I held my breath. She couldn't have heard me. Still on her knees, she swiveled to one side, then the other. She knew that on a dim night like this, it would be sound that would betray her enemy. I began deep tidal breathing, filling my lungs slowly with all the air they could hold.

"PJ, you there?" Daly's voice in my IFB. I couldn't move, couldn't key the radio to answer. "PJ. Acknowledge."

I would have sworn Delia was looking right at me, and for a long moment I imagined her sociopathic roller derby self jumping to her feet, leaping the fence and plunging the knife into my lungs, twisting just for effect, delivering excruciating pain, stealing my life, deflating me until I was gone. I knew she was capable of all of that, and the thought paralyzed me. I doubted I could reach my gun in time. She sniffed the air like an animal and held it. Finally, apparently satisfied that she was alone, she stood to go back into the house.

It was pure reflex that, on my own exhale, my finger came down on the shutter button. It was the mechanical click-click-click that caught her attention.

"Who is it?" she called out. "I know you're there!"

The quiet night sprang to life with barking dogs and porch lights. It took everything in me not to move an inch. Unless she had a flashlight,

I was safe. I didn't think she did, because she hadn't used one yet; and while the beam might be a help to her, it also would betray her location. A person like Delia would be aware of things like that. So I waited again. And she waited. Finally she made a move, backing up slowly, and I thought she was going inside. But she stopped just short of the kitchen door and bent to touch the ground. She came up with a handful of those egg-sized polished river rocks that people use to put a fancy edge on their gardens. She did a Babe Ruth wind-up and used those overdeveloped arms to hurl the rocks at me like it was the last play in a tied Game Seven of the World Series. The stones whistled through the air at eighty miles an hour and showered my forehead and the camera.

Who could prepare for this? I shrieked in pain and shock, and was catapulted straight up as my brain telegraphed to my bent knees *Flex fast and get the hell out of there!* When I landed, I was trapped between snarling predators barreling toward me from opposite directions: Delia coming from just across the fence, and a Rottweiler flying out the back door of the house just behind me, illuminated by a 100 watt porch light that was now fully on.

Delia got there first, with the kitchen knife. The chain links rattled when she hit the fence at full roller derby velocity, with the knife at shoulder height angled directly down at me. She was braced to take the three-foot leap when she saw the dog. The animal was a seventy pound freight train, sure of himself, ears back, head down, glistening eyes locked on my throat. Seconds from impact, I was still on my back. I remember very clearly how the wet, vibrating growl in his throat seemed very personal as he opened his jaws to take the first bite. I pushed off and rolled over, gaining just a few inches. This exposed not my neck, but my head.

I could feel the wind as he slammed into me, and we skidded a good foot and a half across the lawn. His teeth sank without hesitation into my scalp. No, his teeth sank into my wig! The wig, which was not attached to my head because I'd run out of bobby pins, came off and probably saved my life. The dog had ripped away a mouthful of brown hair, and his powerful neck was focused on shaking it to death. An amazing amount of drool was flying everywhere in slow motion. I was spitting out a big blob of it when Delia put it it all together.

"You! PJ Santini, you red headed bitch!" she bellowed. "I know who you are! *This is for you!* You're next, bitch, and I never go back on a promise!" She thrust the knife toward me half a dozen times from six feet away to make her point, willing the tip to pierce my heart. The way she was looking at me, I was surprised her eyes hadn't done that.

I struggled to my feet and recovered the camera; when I looked again, she'd vanished into the night, leaving me to deal with the dog... and with the deeper darkness that was setting in behind my eyes.

The next thing I remembered was the sound of Daly's two-way car radio. All hell was breaking loose. Delia had peeled out in her SUV and was leading Rick on a reckless chase through adjoining neighborhoods. He finally let her go, before some innocent person got hurt. I was slumped beside Daly, strapped into the passenger seat. My head was pounding as blood rushed to my forehead.

"Don't try to talk," he said, searching my eyes for a clue to whether I was going to die right there in the car, looking for pupil dilation that might indicate concussion. "I had to pepper spray the mutt and carry you out. The owner had a revolver in one hand and a phone in the other, dialing your friends at the Precinct." Up until then, I hadn't realized the car was moving; I'd thought all the rocking and swaying was in my head. At least that was good news.

"Where are we?" I asked.

"Dr. Feelgood is going to have a look at you. If he thinks you need the Emergency Room, we're going, don't argue." I always argue, it's what I do. It's humiliating when word gets out that someone's bloodied me up again.

"Why don't you ever tell me Dr. Feelgood's real name?," I asked him. "Is he a real doctor?"

"Of course. Military. Old friend." He stopped there. Asking for more would be pointless, I wouldn't get it. Often he did this for my own protection... a person can know too much. But if Daly trusted him, so did I.

We met him as usual in a parking lot. In my fizzy head I imagined the scene from a distance, me leaning out of the car, hyperventilating behind a WalMart in the middle of the night, with a near-stranger training a military-issue bright flashlight on my face.

"You'll be okay," the doctor finally decided. "Give me your arm, this will relax you." He gave me a shot of something that felt pretty damn good, and handed me a baggie of ice and two Tylenol. "Put this ice on the bruises for the swelling, then I hope you've got some kickass make-up."

"What about the Tylenol?"

"They're for Tango." He glanced sideways at Daly. "You said it was rocks. At this hour. I won't ask."

"You never do." Tango gave him a secret guy nod, and the two cars left the lot by different exits.

CHAPTER NINE

Napoleon Solo didn't show that night, and who could blame him. Napoleon being super hot, he'd want a woman who moaned from pleasure, not from being slammed in the head with landscape rocks. Amazingly, the ice had worked. By morning there wasn't very much swelling on my face, and L'Oreal covered the darkest red marks. The worst calling card Delia had left was the splitting headache hammering behind my eyes. I skipped coffee and went directly to my sartorial comfort zone: black boots with my black turtleneck Catwoman outfit, the sleeveless summer version. And of course, Prada big tortoiseshell sunglasses. Every woman has her default clothes, and these are mine. If push comes to shove, I can throw on a jacket in some nice color that Murray Soper's high paid media consultants would approve of, and go on the air with it. The fact that in this condition I looked like something out of the Star Wars Cantina is beside the point.

I felt my way down to the parking garage and into the Toad, which Daly had somehow spirited home for me. I told the car to drive through Dunkin Donuts for some coffee. Then I let him find his own route to the station, and even park next to Renza. Because the Catsuit doesn't leave much to the imagination, there's no place to stash my Sig. So it was in my clutch purse, which I carried into the station like a football. It was perfectly safe and easy to access. I had taken charge of my own situation. Daly would never know.

I made it to over to my office, half concealed from the newsroom but available enough, if anyone really wanted to look for me. Fiddling with the keys required some effort, since I was determined to keep the sunglasses on. But concentration paid off, and I'd just inserted the glitzy leopard one into the lock when Renza came up behind me.

"PJ! BABE!"

Everything went flying, the keys, the coffee... the purse! I saw it sail down the hall in slow motion, twisting through an airborne eddy of hot coffee, and finally deflecting off the top of the copy machine. At that point, the purse popped open and the Sig sailed out. Ever since the strip joint episode, I'd taken to carrying Daisy cocked but with the safety on, ready for defense. *Safety on. Safety on. It's got to hold!*

"Dive!" I screamed at Renza, and knocked him to the ground.

The gun made a dull sound as it bounced off a wall and thudded down to the carpet. I stopped breathing. Every muscle was tense, bracing for the worst, as the gun lay there staring back at me with its one eye never blinking.

There was no such thing as delayed firing pin action, was there? What if it was playing with me? I was not above backing away from the situation, on my hands and knees if necessary, but I couldn't move.

"Stay," I said to the gun, and looked down to see where I was.

Renza was under me at an angle, gasping with his face sandwiched in between my boobs.

I gave him some breathing air. He winked.

I slapped him. He winked again.

Off to the side, a crowd had gathered. "Place your bets, my friends. Twenty-to-one she keeps him pinned till the noon news. Put your money here." Sports guys'll bet on anything.

"Are you growing a beard?" I asked Renza as we got back on our feet.

"Yep, for awhile. Something different. You like it?"

"No. What does Honey Boo Boo say?"

"Kathy doesn't care what I do. Beardwise, I mean." "Oh really. He winked again. Actually, he looked terrific, but I could never admit it. "Stop the winking. It looks like you've got something in your eye." "Only you, babe, only you." I love hearing him say it even though I know it's bullshit. Truth is, Johnny Renza couldn't be faithful to one woman if his life depended on it. Or if he were offered a million dollars. Or if he were promised a Pulitzer. As none of that is ever going to happen, he figures why even try.

"By the way, how's your head?"

"How do you know about my head?" Nobody would have told Renza about the rock throwing.

"It's on the card that came with a delivery for you this morning. Couldn't help looking. I was just bringing it to you." A few feet away lay the remains of a good size potted plant. It didn't really look like something from a professional florist, more like a personal gift. Sometimes viewers are nice that way. He scooped it off the newsroom carpet and we gave it a home in my office, in the corner by the desk. "Here," he handed me the card.

Heard about your accident last night. Hard head. Careful, it could happen again."

"Did you see who brought this in?" I asked him.

"Yep. Average delivery person." Renza went on to perfectly describe Delia in her plaid shirt, but in the blonde rollergirl wig. Fortunately, she didn't know I'd ever seen it. Static up the back of my neck, because Delia wasn't the charitable kind. This was not good.

"She say anything?" as I plopped down in my nice, new swivel office chair.

Renza started talking but I didn't hear a lot, because the greenery had started shivering. Now the leaves were undulating with a kind of swishing sound. The noise moved steadily, the way a river never rests but keeps on going. He stopped to watch, too, when a head appeared and a forked tongue darted out, followed by a slithering, three-foot-long, tan body with big reddish blotches outlined in black. The snake rustled through leaves around the base of the plant, then headed fast along the baseboard toward the pile of books and papers at my feet.

"Mother of Pearl!" I jumped up. "Call the cops! No, don't call the cops! Call my father!" If 911 were called, Longoria would get wind of it and he'd find a way to use it to get me for something, god knows what. It's the way he thinks. By now he'd probably gotten the sad news that he couldn't tie me to any murders based on the DNA evidence provided by my hair extensions. Sometimes I amaze myself.

Forty-five minutes later, Pop had called in his go-to cop buddy for reptile issues, Oscar Mayer. No, not the hotdog guy. Oscar came over and bravely confronted the snake, hustling it into a cardboard box.

"You weren't in any danger." Oscar leaned on the door jam, peering down the hall. He tried to sound soothing. "It looks like a Coral Snake, but its not. It's an Eastern Milk. They're carnivorous, yeah, and they're constrictors, but they stick to animals they can take. You'd be too big a job."

"That doesn't make me feel a whole lot better."

"It should. Whoever sent it could've used something poisonous, like a Massasauga. Now, there's a snake. They..."

"Okay! Really! Thanks, Oscar, I appreciate it." And I did. "I'll keep you on automatic dial."

"Right. Your dad wants to talk to you. He said to tell you it's the human that's the problem. A different kind of cold blooded predator, that's what he said." And Oscar disappeared out the door, into the parking lot.

Now Renza was intrigued. "What's all this about?" he wanted to know.

Suddenly I was reluctant to tell him. I'd tried repeatedly to fill him in on the backyard bodies story, to tell him what Longoria had inadvertently told me, that there were multiple bodies. Now I was afraid that if

I did, he'd stupidly take it back to Longoria as a question, and Longoria would drag me into it again. So I said nothing. But I did ask something.

"Renza, why did you go to Minsky's house?"

"Why did I go? Why did *you* go?"

"I was just curious. You know I did a story on her, and she just seemed odd to me." That was the truth, just not the whole truth. "But why did you go?"

"Okay, here's the deal. Cornelius left a message on the newsroom general voice mail that his sister was going to kill him. He said he had information about some murders. Frankly, it sounded like a crank call. But when I got hold of it, I went right over. I got there just before you did."

Now I felt like a heel for not giving Renza more info, so I decided to trust him.

"Thanks," I told him, "I appreciate your honesty... although I know you told me in part because I'd find out anyway. Now I'm going to let you in on something, something that the rest of the newsroom doesn't know, something that could hurt me if the source found out that it came from me. Can you keep that part of it secret?"

"Absolutely. I'd never do anything to hurt you, PJ, you should know that. I mean, I don't always act like it, but I do still care about you. Very much." Visions of liasons past danced in my head, memories that spanned decades from out behind the bleachers to family dinners to even a couple of things recent enough for Tango to be jealous. A lot of history. He looked sincere enough. And, as there was zero chance this was a situation in which his sincerity was going to get him laid, I decided to trust him.

"Okay, here goes. Longoria told me personally that there are multiple bodies in backyards in Buffalo. Multiple. Bodies plural." I didn't go so far as to get specific about the one in Willy Short's backyard. "He didn't tell me on purpose. *And you can't mention me in any way, because he'll remember.*"

Renza looked stunned. Maybe he'd had a feeling about it but he couldn't corroborate it. Well, now he could, and we'd have a better story.

"Thanks, Janice." He'd used my high school name.

"You're welcome, Johnny."

Ten minutes later, when I'd almost gotten my breathing under control, Murray Soper tried his luck at getting me to go out on a story. I shot him one of Nonna's *don't even think about it* looks, and he ran into the men's room.

I turned my attention to phone calls I'd missed. Just for me, our telephone receptionist, Cherry Snyder, had replaced the little pink "While You Were Out" message slips with ones that said "While You Were Eating/Sleeping/Shopping". Cherry was still living from gynecological lab test to gynecological lab test, having dated the late, perverted reporter/drug lord Gerald Sigmund. She'd picked up some condition that medical science still couldn't identify, but she'd somehow managed to keep her sense of humor.

A message showed Turner Over had called. I got back to her at the Property Records office.

"Hey Turner, what's up?"

"Hey PJ, just checkin' whether you still want that complete property printout. Maybe Smitty can pick it up."

"Huh? What printout?" So Turner was getting lonesome for Smitty, and manufacturing a little reason to see him. That was so cute.

"You know, the printout of all the properties registered in Delia Minsky's name. Or did you just want the one?"

"You mean there are others?"

"Oh yeah. Let me see... one... two... four... six total. All owned by her. The woman's a land baron."

I was stunned. Delia Minsky? I knew the ordinary looking broad I'd first met was in reality a vengeful, zealous maniac in the derby rink, and she was even capable of killing her own brother; but a landowner not on the skids financially, with a little empire to protect? What was her racket?

"Hell yeah, I want that! Be right there." As a special thank you, I sent Smitty instead. That oughta put a smile on her face.

I hung around the station long enough for Smitty to get back with the Minsky printouts... and a big smile on *his* face. He'd be picking up Turner for a dinner date. I had my own date, at home with a stack of new property information, and I was bracing for the implications.

With government information like this at hand, it would be child's play for Longoria to put it all together. Had he? Or maybe, like me, he still didn't know exactly what he was looking for. Did we at last have something in common? What we would not have in common was this mobbed-up cop's effort to use any little thing to get me out of the way.

For once, Vicky answered without having to pull her head out of the sink. "How well do you know Delia's alter ego, Twisted Sister?" I asked.

"Well, I wouldn't want anybody else to know, but we've chitchatted."

"Oh yeah? About what?"

"Lots of things. She doesn't like it when you get real personal, so I try to keep it light. For instance, I asked about her tattoos. She's got lots of 'em."

"And?"

"She sent me to a guy named Sparky, at Ambush Tattoos over on Steele. She says once you establish a relationship with him, he'll do lots of extra things for you. I liked him. Very clean. As I'm all about getting my money's worth, I'll be going back for more."

I thanked Vicky for the review, and rooted around in my bra drawer for something that would put me in a tattooing mood. Not that I was going to get one; I was just going to pretend to be interested. Red corset? Yes. Under a low-cut top loose enough to conceal the stretchy, wraparound Belly Band holding Daisy. That would go over the corset.

Jeans? No, but a little short skirt. And flip-flops. This was not my favorite look, but somebody in a tattoo parlor might call it bitchin'. I steered over to Steele and crossed into a part of town I try to avoid whenever possible. While there was little chance anyone would risk doing five years for carjacking the Toad, I still locked the doors as I drove. Ambush Tattoos sat on a lot with no trees, no grass, no shrubs. Just an enormous sign with a picture of a bleeding heart and "Get Tattooed at Ambush" across the bottom. The business was the size of a Winnebago. In fact, it was a Winnebago. With a large, empty front parking lot, no humans in evidence, and seven cars lined up at the rear.

At the top of the wooden steps, I opened the front door expecting to see a roomful of people. No one was there, just an area smaller than my walk-in, with a couple of benches along a wall papered with drawings and photos of tattoos. And a piece of cardboard with Ambush Tattoo's business policy in big print: CASH ONLY. Beside it was a small blackboard with prices. $40 would get me a two inch square full-color design. I could choose one I saw, bring one in, or go for pot luck. I decided to say I wanted that Rolling Stones tongue and lip design Janice Soprano had tattooed on her left breast. While Sparky was helping me decide where to put it, I'd pump him for information on Delia.

Drawn curtains to my right separated this waiting area from the business end of the Winnebago. I looked inside, and Sparky was looking back.

"Can I help you, little lady?" Six feet, around a hundred ninety pounds, mostly muscle, deep voice, smoker, Harley rider for sure. Clean jeans that showed off his quads, T-shirt that covered about half his tattoos. They went all the way down to his wrists, and up almost to his jaw. Blue eyes, dark greying hair pulled into a ponytail. About forty. Behind him a sign declared "Nobody here cares how cheap your last tattoo was". The one beside it ordered "No political or religious talk in this shop. Leave your kids at home."

"Hi," I said sweetly, "I'm interested in a tattoo. I think I know what I want, but I could use some advice," and I pointed my bazookas at him.

"No problem. Have a seat," he said to my breasts. He pulled out a clean pair of medical quality gloves to put on. "What size?"

"38 Double-D. Oh, you meant size of... what?"

"The tattoo. What size?"

"Oh, I'll take the two inch square."

"That'll be forty dollars, tax included. Pay now, before I wash up."

But if I paid in advance, how could I get my money back when I said I'd changed my mind? This wasn't Daly's case, so I couldn't exactly write this off to the company. Reluctantly, I pulled out a twenty and two tens, and slid them over to him. He tucked them deftly under the biggest revolver I'd ever seen, sitting at his right elbow.

"So, uh, you have a clientele that's pretty broad? I mean, of broads? I mean, lots of different women?" I asked him.

"Oh yeah, lots." He washed his hands in the sink and followed with disinfecting gel.

"So what tattoo do you want?"

"The Rolling Stones tongue and lip thing. I just don't know where to put it."

He prepared the ink colors and opened fresh needles.

"So... women get tattoos. Princesses? Derbygirls? What?"

I needed information before he started drawing blood.

"As a matter of fact, yeah, derbygirls. Lots of 'em. I give 'em what they want."

"And what do they want? Professionally, of course."

"They like it rough, kinda raw, know what I mean?"

"No, I don't. For example, there's a derbygirl named Twisted Sister. She has lots of tattoos. Know her?"

"You bet," he said proudly. "I do her work."

"Really. So which one is her favorite?"

"It's a hand grenade where her muff should be. Looks really

interesting when she lets the hair grow out." I cringed at the image. "It's got no pin. She's ready to go off any minute." He had no idea. "By the way, Sparky, how'd you get that name?" "Well," he rubbed his crotch, "I've got my own grenades. And you know how unstable they can be when there's no pin and they slam into each other." He sized up my skirt down where Little Janice was getting nervous. "You, uh, you want one?" He feigned an intimacy that
made my skin crawl.

"No thanks. Just make me relax by telling me some nice normal things about good ole hometown rollergirls. Girls like Twisted Sister.
Does the Sister have a brother in real life? I bet they're good friends."

"They hate each other. Anyway, she doesn't come here for family counseling. She has money to burn, and she spends it on elaborate tattoos. Every inch of her body has got something on it. Believe me, I know." His eyes traveled south to my skirt again. You sure I can't do something for you down there? We could maybe put the tongue low enough to enjoy itself," as he reached to lift the hem.

"Oh, look at the time." I glanced at the spot on my wrist where my watch would've been if I'd remembered to put it on. Standing while he was sitting, he didn't look so formidable. I was mapping out the quickest route to my money, when he read my mind.

"I'll just hold onto this for you, little girl," he said, patting the cash. You come on back whenever you're ready."

The only thing I was ready for was to get the hell out.

THE TOAD AND I WERE retracing our tracks out of the hood, taking corners on two wheels and calculating how many tanks of gas that wasted forty dollars would have bought, when Pop called. He'd just gotten word the nude remains had been identified. I hit the brakes and swerved to a stop in the first available place, the sidewalk of a window-less purple adult fun house called *Laddie's*. Nothing ever turned out well for me anywhere near strip clubs, but I had no choice.

"It's a biker dude whose estranged wife has been looking for him for a year. He was wrapped in a bedspread from a big chain cheapo motel. The guys in Homicide think the murders are related, because in every case a little something was left behind."

"Like what?" I asked Pop.

"Like traces of some sorta makeup."

"So these guys liked to doll up? They were cross dressers?"

"That ain't the part of the body where the makeup was."

"Where, then?"

"An' it's not flesh-colored..."

"Where, Pop?"

"Lower. An' it's white."

"Pop, for god's sake, how much low... Oh...my...god!"

"I'm pretty sure your mother's Birds And Bees talk she had with you when you turned thirteen didn't cover this, but I think you get it."

That's not all I got. The only person I ever knew who wore white makeup was the same person who'd just murdered her own brother in cold blood, shot him squarely in the chest. If Pop knew that, if he knew she'd nearly carved me up with a butcher knife and promised to finish the job, he'd go ballistic.

"Where are you, Pop? Can Ma hear this?"

"Probably, I'm in the living room now."

I couldn't hold back the tears and couldn't find a Kleenex. "Hold on." I blew my nose into a map of Upper New York State.

"This is so fucked up, I don't know where to start," I wailed, "and I don't want Ma to know! Or Nonna or Tony or Vicky or Sandro. They'll all try to help." I didn't have to remind my father that Sandro, a New

Jersey Pit Bull in a shiny suit, *lives* to deliver attitude adjustments. A lot has gone unsaid in our house.

And Nonna, the Sicilian righter of all wrongs, is legendary. She still isn't allowed back into the idyllic little cemetery next to the St. Agatha of Catania church, after one of the ladies from the Old Country died. It was the one who Nonna consistently beat at Monday night gin, Tiziana Testolina . The woman swore revenge when she passed into the next life. Lo and behold, her *Gorgonzola*-clogged arteries gave way one night, in the middle of a terrible storm. In her last moments, Tiziana shook her fists at the heavens as Beethoven is said to have done, and as lightning flashed swore to exact revenge on Nonna.

Nonna, being a believer in prevention rather than cure, decided to head that off. By the dark of the moon on the night they buried Tiziana, Nonna Giovanna Santini filled a 10-gallon orange-and-white Igloo drink container with a potent "cleansing potion" of water and a ton of sea salt and, with Tony's reluctant help, drenched Tiziana's grave and the surrounding area. That should keep her at bay.

As it happened, Tiziana also grew prize-winning roses, the finest of which had been carefully transplanted that very morning to her final resting place. By noon of the next day, thanks to the salt, it looked like a UFO had landed and sucked up all the color, and every living thing, in a fifty-foot radius.

But back to Pop, who wanted to know why his news about the dead guys with the white powder on their privates was shaking me up. He wanted to know the personal connection.

"Aw geez, Pommie, did you find another one?" He was practically whispering. "It'll be awright, just come out and say it. You and bodies have a knack for turnin' up in the same place at the same time."

The thought made me nauseous. It was summer in Buffalo, but I was freezing. Chills were digging into the back of my neck. I checked to make sure Daisy was still in her belly band. Good girl.

"No, nothing to report yet," I sniffled. It wasn't exactly a lie, I just wasn't reporting it. "I've got to go over some paperwork at home this afternoon. Might even help you crack a Cold Case or two."

I shifted around in the car seat and hooked a finger onto my thong to move the damn thing anywhere but where it was. When I get really agitated, my underwear stops fitting. I don't know why. Any minute now, my bra would be too tight.

"By the way, Pop, what around the house did Ski Mask touch? His name's Neely, but I bet you already knew that."

"Well now," he said as he brought his voice back up, "you're right. Steuben Neely, Wristshot. You and I think do alike. Dere's good news and bad news about that. Nonna says he wasn't wearing gloves, that's the good news. The bad news is that your mother got into a cleanin' mood and wiped down everything with Lemon *Pledge*. Right now I'm smellin ' the big family picture frame to see if she got to it yet." I could hear my father sniffing like the Weimaraner, nose-to-nose with an ancient sepia-toned photograph of somber adults and children from the Old Country lined up like deer caught in the headlights, nobody looking very happy.

"Any luck?"

"Bingo. I'll dust and get back to you."

I PARKED IN MY RESERVED, secured space under Erie Towers, telling myself I was safe at last, and deep in thought about the white makeup on Delia's victims' private parts. Was it just me, or was my short skirt getting even shorter? Things were getting so weird that even other residents were starting to feel threatening. As I walked to the elevator they were still watching after I'd passed. One little kid stopped by his car.

"Mommmmmie?" he said, staring at me.

"I know, get in," his mother slammed the door.

By now I was one big goosebump of anxiety, which had dimpled the skin of my thighs into oatmeal. Inside the corset, my nipples were life-size replicas of those erasers you stick on the ends of pencils in school. I made it upstairs, and rummaged around in the kitchen for some whiskey for a good, strong Irish coffee, without the coffee. Which I would take into a hot bath, which would lull me into enough of a calm to tackle the stack of property records on the dining table.

An ugly thought was taking shape: Delia owned lots of houses. Was there a body at every house she owned? Why? At which one was she planning to plant me? Had she already dug the hole?

CHAPTER TEN

While the water was running and Daisy was standing guard, I pulled the "Nurture PJ" box from under the bed. This is the Cavalry of Self-Help, an extreme-measures collection of pampering, reserved for overwhelming moments that are a mere step above thumbsucking in a corner with a raincoat over my head.

It's a big, round rose-colored hatbox papered with Renaissance angels. Inside, there are amber light bulbs and pink ones, Godiva chocolate truffles, beautiful teeny bottles of French liqueur, fragrant foamy bubble bath, decadent oversized Millefleur soap bars, a Mozart "relax" CD, rich body creme and, okay, Ativan. After all, that's what they make it for, right? And a super-soft fringed throw that's as comforting to clutch as a life raft, but far more soothing.

I went shopping in the Box, de-stressed in the tub, slathered on thick, creamy body lotion and bundled into a soft robe to head for the dining room.

Another magnificent breeze off the lake, and afternoon turned to evening. With the sliding glass doors open and the bottle of mystery wine on the dining table practically pouring itself, I'd been through the property reports over and over, and couldn't understand how Delia could have thought she could get away with posing on camera as a poor single homeowner with no assets. It was so easy to check. But then, I'd missed it myself. When the time was right, I'd relish telling the alleged news director that, wherever he got Delia's name for the sob story, he'd been had.

Turner was right, there were more residential single family dwellings listed in her name:

20107 Dianna Rd.

139 Hammersmith St.

24 Macduff Ln.

6691 St. Simeon Dr.

1281 Wing St.

Property taxes on all of them were up to date; no liens. She owned them all free and clear. Cornelius owned nothing.

They both lived at 24 Macduff Lane. Or they did, until Cornelius came up short against her gun. She'd probably used a silencer, since Pop said no shots had been called in. But she apparently hadn't intended to bury him there. Why not? No vacancy in the garden?

1281 Wing St. was where Willy Short lived. A body was there, out by the Queen Anne's Lace.

139 Hammersmith St. was where she was fishing around in the dark with a butcher knife and a shovel and river rocks. After that night, it had come to me that maybe she had intended to bury him there after all, but only part of him, because of his size. It was possible.

The other two addresses meant nothing to me. Should I tell Pop? I poured more wine, scooped up the glass, and went into the bathroom. In front of the mirror, I asked the question again, out loud. *Be honest. Why don't you want to tell Pop?*

Because, I answered deliberately, *I want to figure this out myself. I want to beat the bitch myself, I want to solve it, to beat Renza to the story, to beat Longoria to... everything.*

You're an idiot! You'll get killed, then where will you be?

I took a long sip of whatever I was drinking.

Oh yeah, I also want to... I forget. No, I remember... I want to show Daly how good an investigator I am, not just another pretty face.

I made it to the toilet in time, and spent the next half hour on the pot with my head in my hands wondering what the hell to do next.

IT WAS 4 AM BEFORE I finally got to sleep, there was so much on my mind. The phone rang at the crack of noon. Ma sounded so cheerful, I knew it was a plea for help.

"Good morning, Pommie. I was just thinking, Nonna Giovanna and I have been spending so much quality time together, it's a pity you have to miss out on it."

"Huh?" I hadn't even had coffee yet.

"Well, remember when you were stuck in that My Apartment strip club not so long ago, and you made a vow - I don't know to which saint, maybe just to god in general - that if you got out of there alive, you'd take me to lunch every week, and Nonna too?"

"Uh huh."

"Now, I never held you to that, of course. But today would be a good day to start."

"Uh huh."

"If we don't," she whispered fast, "your grandmother is going to join a motorcycle gang. Too much free time. Help!"

In the background I could hear Pop. "For da last time, Ma, you can not go to the store in a biker helmet that says *I'VE GOT PMS AND I'M ARMED* on the front and SHUT THE FUCK UP on the back! You just don't do that in Lovejoy!"

"Well, atsa what they do in Sicily!" Nonna shot back.

"No, they do not!" he bellowed before the screen door slammed. "Dey don't do it!" Pop repeated from somewhere on the front lawn.

"Gotcha, Ma," I told her.

Nonna picked up the extension, "I'ma gonna wanna go to that nice restaurant by your condo, the one with the marvelous selection of delectable items too numerous to mention."

"You mean the Goose and Gander, the lunch buffet?" I asked.

"I hear the crab legs are to die for."

I was waiting for them in the parking lot, when Ma's old Chevy pulled up. The back door creaked open and a pair of clunky black oxfords slid toe-first down to the pavement. Thick black cotton stockings ran up to a long black rayon dress that only a nun would wear in this heat. Or Nonna. In her neighborhood, the old Sicilian dress code kicked in somewhere around the age of forty: all black, all the time. Her shawl was pulled up to her grin.

"*A cane?*" I said to Ma, as Nonna waved a stick with a tortoise shell handle. "The woman's a mountain goat, she goes up and down the stairs all the time. Since when did she start carrying a cane?"

"Since she heard it's not a prosecutable lethal weapon. Apparently in Palermo even eighty year olds feel naked without their shotguns , and who's gonna let her have one in Buffalo."

We filed into the Goose and Gander. It was a classic restaurant. Padded booths, nice tables with white cloths, real place settings with weighted knives, windows floor to ceiling. You could hear the chef in the kitchen body slamming the veal for the evening meal. Best of all, it was so close to my condo that if you had field glasses, you could look across the marina up six stories into my corner bedroom.

Sharing a table with Nonna is always an experience. She's the only adult in the room in a booster seat, which she occupies like a throne.

Wednesday is the universal Oldsters' Day Out, and half of elderly Buffalo and their adult kids were sitting here. The waitress smiled down on Nonna and recited the menu as if she were talking to a five year old, nice and slow so nobody would miss anything. Three soup selections including French onion. (Smile) Green salad bar. (Smile) Pickled or creamed herring salad. (Smile) Thin-sliced smoked salmon...

Nonna started to squirm. "And?"

Four vegetable side dishes. Including oven-roasted new potatoes. And let's see, cauliflower baked with two kinds of cheese...

Nonna's head lowered, and when it came up she'd turned on the Manson lamps. The waitress seemed not to notice this dangerous turn of events. "And let's see, a table of delicious desserts ranging from Key Lime Pie to Black Forest Cake to Napoleons to... oh, what's wrong dear,?" she asked, patting Nonna's shoulder, "Are we feeling a little tired today? Would you like some tea?"

"I'll tell ya what's wrong. No fuckin' crab legs? No sumptuous peel 'n' eat shrimp? What the hell?"

It was the lunch that would live in infamy, and we hadn't even asked for water yet. There were no crab legs today, and somehow we all lived past that. There was plenty of shrimp. And Black Forest Cake, which Nonna insisted with wide-eyed innocence and a firm grip on a knife was really a Sicilian invention. The wait staff agreed, and backed off.

Ma gave me the secret wink as I paid the tab at the register. She appreciated the break. And then the shit hit the fan.

Nonna was standing inside the air conditioned Goose and Gander, waiting for us, gazing through the front door at the waves of heat floating off the baking-hot parking lot, when she went "Huh." She leaned in and put her nose to the glass, exhaled on it, wiped it dry with her shawl, and pronounced, "That looks a lot like Sweet Boy."

"What does?" Ma said as she dug in her purse for a Kleenex.

"That."

The three of us stared out in utter disbelief.

"Yes, it does," Ma whispered

"Yes, it is," I whispered back.

We watched the car for a full minute, as if it were a bird and might fly away at the slightest movement, before we eased the restaurant door open. I checked the parking lot. Nobody was going to or from the car, in fact no one was around at all. To confirm what I already knew, I knelt and checked for the red nail polish heart I'd drawn under the front bumper. There it was. My own heart was pounding.

"It is you! Oh, I've missed you so much!" I kissed his back fender, and the Mercedes symbol on the trunk. The trunk! Sweet Boy was, unbelievably, unlocked. I guess if you steal a car and drive it uninsured, what's to lose. He looked to be in great shape, but who knew. The trunk popped open on command and my wigs were still there, underneath a dirty t-shirt that said "*Yo bitch this 1's for you*", only the 1 wasn't really a number, just a dildo, how clever. There was a roll of paper towels, a five pound bag of cornmeal, and a half-drunk big bottle of flat Coke. There were cigarette ashes on the front seat. I wondered if this was the actual person who had stolen my SLK from in front of the My Apartment strip joint while I was working the Sigmund case. I wanted to get my hands on the bastard.

A sane person would call the cops.

Ma was already calling Pop, the same thing. "Dominic, you'll never guess what. Pommie's SLK is over here at the restaurant! Yep, we just came outside and here it is! Pretty good, looks good. Okay, you do that. Hurry!"

"Your father's on the way over, Pommie. He's visiting some friends at the police station." Ma was talking to me the way that waitress had talked to Nonna, calmly and slowly, trying to keep a lid on the situation. "He reporting it. And he says to let air out of the tires before the driver comes back. And to stay out of trouble."

A sane person would do that, and wait for the cops.

Nonna, on the other hand, said she'd cover me at the front door, and on a hunch I went around to the kitchen swinging the "*Yo bitch this 1's for you*" t-shirt over my head and burst in the back door yelling "Who's the limp dick who's dreaming THIS big! Huh? Who is it?"

This threw the entire kitchen into chaos, prompting one person in particular, the dish washer with arms in dirty water up to his elbows, to come at me full-tilt and slam me into a refrigerator. He got his footing and hurled himself through a steaming maze of boiling vats of seafood, then expertly rode a rolling stack of trays loaded with Napoleons until it crashed into a wall. I took off after him, skating on icing, and didn't fall only because I had one of the chefs by his starched white shoulders.

By the time the dish washer hit the swinging double doors into the dining room, the chef was fishing his hat out of a lobster pot. I went through the doors myself, and clipped the waitress who was just leaving our table, loaded down with the Bloody Mary glasses and Irish Coffee cups.

"Next time a much bigger tip!" I panted, and I'm pretty sure she flipped me off. I could see how waiting on a testy Sicilian grandmother could make a person cranky. "Heads up, Nonna!" I belted out. The jackass had just rounded the corner to the lobby.

He heaved the door open and Nonna swung her cane toward his shins. Whap! He went down screaming. She launched into unintelligible curses, pointing several fingers at his private parts. He wasn't Italian, he was from Jamaica, but he knew danger when he saw it, and stopped fighting.

"Come on," she says, "come on, show me whatta you got," making palms up, open-closed hand movements encouraging him to get up, bouncing around like a boxer.

The senior citizen lunch crowd spilled out to watch, snapping cell phone pictures, disagreeing over whether this was for real or some sort of new restaurant gimmick.

He struggled to his feet and went for Nonna's throat. But she was faster. She stepped away and started spinning with that cane. After three or four turns she was a little off-balance, but still managed to plant a direct hit on his butt, sending him down face first.

Next, the sure sign a Santini is involved: sirens. The responding patrolman, in his early twenties, had never seen anything like this. He wanted to cuff the guy, but first he had to call off the black whirlwind, and this wasn't something they taught at the Academy.

About that time, Pop arrived. In all my years, I'd never known he could whistle like that. "C'mon Ma! Mom! Nonna!" He tried them all, then the whistle. She stopped immediately. She straightened her shawl, smoothed her skirt, and marched back to Ma's Chevy. It was like having a killer robot.

I glanced over at Pop, who was standing by Sweet Boy, giving him the once-over. Then he ducked out of sight. By the time I got there, he was back on his feet. He gave me a big hug.

"I did the right thing," he said mysteriously. "Sometimes what my little girl doesn't know can hurt her."

The rest of the day was spent on cop shop stolen car paperwork, insurance company stuff, getting what had been a mint condition Mercedes SLK back looking like somebody cared again, and saying a bittersweet goodbye to the Toad. I know this sounds crazy, but that ugly green car had been dependable, and certainly had contributed to my anonymity at a time when it was pretty important. The Sigmund case had involved murder, drugs, and the mob. Flying under the radar in the Toad had not been such a bad idea. And now, Sweet Boy was back. Endings and beginnings.

Day drifted into evening, and I was just crashing at home when Daly called.

"It's done."

"What's done?" I asked. I'd already told him about Sweet Boy.

"What we talked about before. It's done. Now it's someone else's problem."

The diamond had been passed to Wristshot! So much relief in one day. The car back in my life. The diamond, and the jerk who came with it, out.

"Thank you, Tango. Really, thank you! And thank Rick."

"No problem. Call you back in a couple of hours. I was up all night on a case, and I'm going to sleep awhile." I blew him a kiss.

Sleep seemed like a pretty good idea. It would take a calmer mind to figure out what to do about about Delia. With all the draperies pulled, outside doors locked, and the air conditioning turned down to *Cover up before you freeze,* I let hibernation set in. Around eleven I came to, with teeth chattering. The sleep had been solid. My cell phone showed a missed call and a voice message. It was Wristshot Neely.

"I got your message. As a thank you, I have something for you, something Lou wanted you to have. It's not safe for us to meet in the open. Meet me at the Olde Town Cemetery at 2 AM. Gate'll be unlocked. Follow the path around to the big mausoleum with two dark angels on top. Look through the iron bars on the door and you'll find it."

First thought: call Daly. But no, he needed his sleep. And I was a big girl. Neely wasn't a threat anymore, he had what he wanted, and I couldn't imagine why he'd want anything else from me. Maybe we'd even shake hands and move on. I know, that's crap, but I was trying.

I decided to go. But what do you wear to a cemetery when you're just sort of, you know, there on business? Black, out of respect. But slacks only, any more would be too depressing. And a white pullover shirt. And flats... heels just didn't seem right. Plus, they reminded me of the way my stilettos sank into the earth at Siggy's funeral, the very day Wristshot surfaced.

I took Sweet Boy out on the old east highway until the neighborhoods fell away and it was mostly country. Somewhere in the stillness a church clock struck two, and the sound echoed off my closed car windows as I positioned the SLK in the shadows by the gate. The closest building to the cemetery, a bar across the street called The Last Stop, had locked up at midnight. The owner was famously superstitious about doing business on this otherwise deserted road past the witching hour. Of course, with my Sicilian heritage I don't get the whole negative witch thing. Neither does Nonna, who is constantly grinding plants and burning them in pots around the house for protection. The last time she did that in the garage, where Pop has the lawnmower fuel stored, she almost blew up the house. I did what Neely had said, and hoped I was at the right mausoleum. Squinting through the iron grate, I waited for my eyes to adjust to the dark. Even though the pupils were wide open, they couldn't pick up a thing. I angled in for a better view, and the door gave way. The screech of the reluctant metal hinges made my teeth hurt all the way up to the sinuses. *Daisy, are you there?* I felt around for the Sig. *You bet your ass,* she answered from her home in the elastic bellyband around my abdomen, under my shirt. *And your cell phone's right beside me.*

Of course! I could use the flashlight on my cell! I inched the door open a little more, vowing to pack WD40 the next time, *god don't let there be a next time,* and held the phone at arm's length. When I finally found the button on the touch screen, the beam was so strong I tried to minimize it and fumbled the damn thing. Next thing I knew, I was on my hands and knees groveling around in decades of filth. Panicked and feeling ridiculous, scraping my fancy Big Apple Red nail polish through caked dirt and wet something, I finally got my hands on the phone and shined it in front of me.

In the brightness, a frozen vision of Lou floated before me. *Lou! But this is impossible!* He didn't move, he just looked at me.

CHAPTER ELEVEN

Lou! What're you doing here! I mean, of course this would be where you would be, being deceased and all. I was trying to reason with my dead husband, with whom I couldn't reason when he was alive. This was on the inside. On the outside:

"Aaaaaaaaaaaaahhhh!" The sound didn't bounce off the walls. The stone mausoleum absorbed it, which was in no way comforting. This meant if I screamed louder, if that were even possible, no one would hear. I'd never felt more completely alone.

My brain struggled to create an explanation. He wasn't merely vapor, like ghosts in movies. He was solid, real. Lou Bonmarito in the flesh, my brain said. Combed, perfect hair. Amused half-smile. Pressed shirt, nice suit, shined shoes. But why wouldn't he move, why wouldn't he give me that much? He was so one-dimensional. He was so... cardboard. A life-size cardboard standup.

If human brain neurons normally fire two hundred times a second, what does adrenaline do to them? My head was lit up like a pinball machine with the Tilt light flashing. Husband, no husband... real, not real. Processing the newest incoming data was even harder now, because the corroded hinges on the door behind me had begun an intermittent squealing, and as this was not a windy night this was not a good sign.

"You're such an idiot," the voice said softly. My thoughts exactly. Only an idiot would come to a cemetery alone, on the advice of a wacked-out stranger.

"Hands in the air," he said, and I followed orders. "Turn around. Easy does it." My flashlight beam cut through the dark as I moved, across cobwebs, a holy water font, the face of Wristshot Neely, and the .38 he was aiming at my chest.

"This is what you told me about? This is what Lou wanted me to have? You have the diamond now, so what's the point?"

"You know too much."

"But I trusted you!"

"Walk in front of me, head back where you came from, but take a right at the first path."

This was bad. I walked slowly, calculating the odds of taking him by surprise if I doubled over and swung around. A clumsy effort would be better than nothing. But his footsteps didn't sound close enough. Maybe I could just make a break for it and hide behind a tombstone. I did have Daisy and a spare magazine.

"Don't even think about it," he said. I don't mind shooting you. It's only a question of how far to drag the body." He was right. Killing me there would be like rolling out pastry dough in a bakery. It was the perfect spot, what else would you do there?

"Maybe we can work something out," I told him, breathing deeply, slowly, sending oxygen to the muscles, getting ready. *Watch it. Don't let him focus on the next thing. We all know what the next thing is.*

"Too late, the potty's over."

Who knows what makes a woman lose control. A thought, maybe a phrase... a word.

"Potty! What is it with you? From the very beginning, you and the cod, you and the nice tits sweethot. What is it with you? Speak English!" I yelled, whipping around like a windmill with the really powerful straight-arm open-hand strike Tango Daly had taught me, the one I swore I'd never need. My palm made contact with the side of his head with enough force to knock him off his feet. I ran like hell back toward the car. Navigation never being my strong suit, I was still leaping around grave markers long after I should have been there. *Where's the fence, is there even a damn fence?*

Are gravestones alphabetized? They should be alphabetized. Would they run front to back or back to front? I was crouched in the good size family plot of the Wheelers, doubled over with a side stitch and a desperate need for oxygen. Praying the illuminated screen of the iPhone wouldn't give me away, I whispered to Siri.

"Call Tango Daly".

"Calling Wei To Go," she belted out.

"No, not WEI To Go! Call TANG-O!" I hissed.

"Calling Wei To Go."

"Oh hell, call Operations, bitch!"

"That's not nice..." she said smoothly.

"She's right, it's not," he said from behind me. "Get up."

"I can't," I told him. It was almost true. My knees were knocking.

"Now." In the deathly quiet, the cold metal sound of the hammer cocking. "*Now*". He fired two rounds into the ground.

"Yup, will do," I got to my feet, couldn't bear his stare. "But," I said over my shoulder, "aren't you even going to buy me dinner, first?" The only thing I hadn't tried was humor. No answer. "Okay then, tell me this, why did Delia kill her brother?" He wasn't shocked at the question.

"What the hell, you're dying anyway. I'll tell you. Pictures and blackmail, a natural combination. Somebody's always doing something wrong, everywhere you look. It started way before the Grey Goose Polaroid thing. She did all the work, handled all the cash. We all ate off it. But then she wanted to sell the house and live alone. What was Cornelius supposed to do? No more money, no more cruises. All the records were strictly off-computer, only handwritten by her, so he was going to give them to a reporter or to the cops, and rat her out. She had to kill him."

"What about you?" I slowed the pace, looking for another chance to make a move. "What's in it for you?" Keep him talking. "Walk faster." He took a deep breath. "For me, the real cash is the Grey Goose. Lou was my friend. It was our plan. It was my plan. I was the one who killed the lights at the show, to cause confusion. An' after all that, he swore he'd be able to sell the rock, but he couldn't do it. Now it's my turn. *I will do it.*"

He was feeling pretty proud of himself, taking advantage of his one opportunity to say it all and take credit before an audience who wouldn't live to repeat it.

"Stupid Cornelius and Delia never suspected me at all, but they sure drained ole Lou dry. Then, before you guys went to Maui, Lou wanted me to know the diamond was in the cat, in case anything happened to him before he got back. Which it did."

We walked in silence for about fifty more yards. He wasn't making the mistake of being so close, this time. I would have to decide what to do when we stopped. He didn't know I was armed. This gave me an option, if not an actual advantage, if only I could engineer it out of my clothes. As we moved along the path, I'd lifted almost all of the front of my shirt out of the waistband, then...

"Stop here." Damn. "Oh look," he motioned off to the right, "your table is waiting."

There was no table. About a hundred feet into a mess of stone markers, there was a slab with a lighted lantern on top of it, throwing uneasy shadows over disturbed earth.

That's it! Daisy was vibrating. *Enough already! Pull the damn trigger!* I explained to her that it wasn't that easy. We'd never had words before, but she did have a point. My chances weren't going to get any better. Like Daly says when he speaks to groups of women about basic personal safety, you're always better off fighting off a kidnapper from the get-go, than allowing yourself to be taken somewhere else. This situation exactly. This was Wristshot's scene. His plan, his place. His control would only tighten as the seconds went by. I hated that I was wishing I'd let Daly know I was coming here. It wouldn't have been a weakness. After all, even cops work in pairs.

We walked through the headstones. Suddenly it became terribly important to remember the names on all of them. In a way, it was taking note of landmarks on a strange road, or dropping breadcrumbs, a measure of where I was, where I had been. And, I suppose, it was partly because these might be the last things I ever saw. The names of real people carved into stone for strangers like me to see.

Way too soon, we arrived at the open grave. The angle of the lantern light threw the hole into shadow, and my mind went to work on the questions the living always ask: *How deep is it? What difference does it make? But I need to know.*

My brain was trying to reconcile the six feet under lore with the fact that the top of what was probably a weathered six-foot ladder was sticking out a good foot.

So it can't be six feet deep.

But if you can't crawl out, what difference does it make?

"Get in," he said.

Stall. Stall for time. Say anything.

"Wow, you did all this for me?"

"Not really, it was already dug up for a new occupant in the morning. But this is it. It's gone on too long, already."

"But why? You hold all the cards. You probably have more copies of the Polaroid, and the stupid memory card, and *you have the diamond.*"

"I know I do. It's sitting on that box over by the lamp. I take it everywhere."

"Then just let me go. I won't hold it against you. If I'd worked for Cornelius, I would've gone mental, too."

"Nice try. But there's too much stick handlin', dealing with you."

"Stick handlin'? Speak English. You're not in Boston anymore."

"Yeah, but I'm always on the ice. Means you're too much trouble."

I saw an opening, here. We could change the subject to anything but killing me.

"Ha! I bet you can't even play hockey." No self respecting New Englander would let that go unchallenged.

"Can, too."

"Oh yeah? What position?"

"Right Wing."

"Big deal. Bet you never landed a decent slapshot." I had a feeling a guy who called himself Wristshot did it because he couldn't nail a slapshot goal if the net were 20 feet across.

"Wrong! The wristshot is what makes the game!" I was right. He had issues.

"Is not!"

"Is too!"

"Is not! It's all about the wristshot! You're wrong! Wrong! Wrong!" He was sweating, losing concentration.

""In your dreams. Prove it."

His eyes went blank. The only other time I'd ever seen that was when a guy was... but I digress. He looked around. No hockey sticks. If there were any, considering our location they'd say Buffalo Sabres instead of Boston Bruins, and that would only make him madder. He scratched his head with the barrel of his gun.

"Thought so," I told him, "all show, no go."

"What'd you say?" He gave me a murderous look and moved a step closer. I might have gone too far.

"Look, you haven't committed murder. Stop before you do."

He didn't buy it. "Down there. Now." He motioned with the gun.

I took one last look around and didn't see the Cavalry coming. Shit. Was this how it all was going to end?

They say that when you're near death, you can have a sort of out-of-body experience. I saw myself at a distance - PJ the fighter, PJ the angel, PJ the bitch. In a minute all that wouldn't matter, she would be gone.

She was lowering into nothingness. The wooden ladder dug splinters into my hands.

The unexpected pain brought me back into the present, back into hope, back into terror. *Wake up! You don't want to die! Do you want them to find you in an ordinary shirt and loafers?*

But that's not what I'm wearing.

Close enough. It got you to listen to me, didn't it?

Yes, it did. All was not lost. I could, well, I could do something, I just wasn't sure what. *Pay attention to where you're going, down there. Get Daisy.*

I pulled at the gun and brought her up to aim anywhere above me. *Don't waste ammunition. Be sure of what you're doing.* And count. He's fired two, so he has three left. All he needs is one.

In the instant that it took to glance down and double-check the spare magazine out of habit, there was a loud *Boink!* at ground level.

A human shape was picking up speed overhead, and the heaviness of its warm body knocked me off the ladder and pinned me to the earth below.

"What the fuck! Get offa me! Help!" I was about twenty heart-beats away from an exploded blood vessel.

With strength I didn't know I had, I pushed it off and scrambled up the rungs, head and shoulders in fresh air.

And there stood Willy Short and his shovel.

"I had to, Miss Santini." Willy was feeling gravity-challenged after an evening with Jim Beam, but he was doing okay, and I was never so happy to see him. He was aware enough to notice me trying to make sense of the blood I was wiping off my face.

"I wouldn't worry," he said, "it's not yours."

"It's not? Then whose is it?"

"I saw what he was gonna do to you. You and Mr. Daly were the on-ly people who really listened to me, who didn't think I was crazy. So..."

His insteps were balancing over the edge of the grave and he was fascinated, concentrating on that.

"So?" I prodded.

"So the guy took a shovel hard to the head. Sure hope the cops don't come."

"Sure hope they do."

"Well, I'll be going now."

From out of nowhere, a familiar chilling voice cut through the relief that had flooded my body.

"No," it said. "You won't."

Delia the Twisted, the mother of all madness, was at graveside, in black from head to toe, with full chalky derby makeup.

"So this is the Grey Goose I've heard so much about." She made a show of holding it up as if she could see a damn thing in the dark. "Y'know, bitch Santini, Cornelius's greedy errand boy is even greedier than me! I knew if I watched him long enough, I could nail him.

"Little weenie was moving in on my action. Until he came along, Cornelius and I were making a good chunk o' change. It was so easy. Cornelius set it up, took the pictures whenever, I kept the books, the marks paid. If they got tired of paying or caused trouble I just recycled 'em into a nice Wildlife Habitat backyard garden for the kiddies to play in, so smooth not even my own brother knew what was going on.

"Then stupid Cornelius thought he was dying, and he tried to shoehorn his way into heaven by giving your husband the Polaroid. This knocked off a very significant income stream. Then ol' Wristshot saw more potential for himself, and stole our memory card to go after the diamond.

"And look at this, now. I got *him*, I got *you*, and I got *the diamond too.*" Delia put the Grey Goose down to take aim with both hands.

She couldn't decide who to shoot first. She was literally drooling with excitement, and wiped the slop off her mouth with the back of her wrist, bleeding red lipstick down into the chalky white. If she'd spent all day in Paramount Studios Makeup, she couldn't have looked more like she'd just torn through raw meat. Which didn't steady my nerves. She took aim at Willy, then at me, then at Willy again.

"Diamond. Diamond?" said Willy in a long sigh. He didn't recognize his own landlady and had peed himself a huge one at the very sight of Zombie Delia. "Ho geez, I gotta give up the juice. This is the worst." He unzipped.

"Too late!" Delia's hysterical laughter sliced through the night in wave after wave, higher and higher. She was very close to some sort of mind-blowing orgasm I'd only read about.

Embarrassed, Willy teetered forward to work on zipping back up, and lost his balance. He came straight down on top of Neely's body, causing Neely's limp arm to fly up and smack him in the head. Willy fought it off bravely and somehow surfaced with the guy's gun. This would have been good news if Willy had been lucid enough, at any moment in the last thirty days, to take accurate aim at anything.

Delia was having the time of her life, howling in the dark. She fired one off straight into the air, then turned the muzzle toward the hole.

"Don't shoot," I yelled at Willy. "Duck!" as if he had anywhere to go. He fired anyway, at nothing in particular, and missed everything. Bullets were flying, and it was impossible to keep track of spent rounds. I was still on the ladder and took a shot topside at what I hoped was Delia.

She sprinted toward the shrubbery, and the flickering lantern caught her blonde wig going down into a row of low junipers as a single shot rang out.

Then nothing.

This, I was thinking, would be a damn good time to make a run for it. I scrambled out of the hole and sprinted away, head back, lungs working hard. When I saw a big enough headstone, I threw myself flat on the ground behind it. Mouth full open against the grass, gasping for air and sucking in damp ground and bugs. When I finally looked up, with steadier breathing, there was not one sound. No footsteps. Not even a night creature.

Safe.

Another minute. Listen.

Silence.

Safe.

Then the stirring of a wisp of breath.

"Come here often?"

"Aaaaaahhhhh!" When your hair reaches for the sky like Bill the Cat's, your body goes with it. I was still on the way up when strong hands jerked me down and sealed off my mouth.

"Easy, baby," Tango said. "Take it easy."

I bit his hand and reached over my shoulder to dig my nails into whatever I could find. "Why are people always putting their hands over my mouth! Are you insane? My heart's beating like a jackrabbit!"

"Oh, *the passion*. Try to remember that later."

I was formulating my smart comeback when the sirens began.

A police monitor is a tool of the trade. People who care about it leave it on 24/7. Depending on who's listening, it's a lead to a news story, or to an arrest, or to a life saved. Buffalo Police Department radio dispatch from that morning:

02:20:49 hrs: Report of gun shots several minutes ago at Olde Town Cemetery east of town. Repeat: multiple shots fired at Olde Town Cemetery. All available units respond.

At 02:20:50 hrs, Pop was already on his way because of the tiny Student Driver Tracking Unit he'd intended to put on the Toad, but wound up putting on Sweet Boy instead, because he'd had it with him the day the SLK showed up again. He'd made a solemn vow to keep his daughter's lost privacy to a minimum, with alerts to go to him only if her car left Buffalo proper. In the Goose and Gander parking lot, he'd dropped down and popped the Unit's magnetic holder on Sweet Boy's underside. Just a few minutes ago, the Unit had sent an *Outside Speci-*

fied Area alert and he'd jumped in the car in his jammies and started driving. When he heard the radio dispatch call, he hit the gas and phoned Iroquois Investigations.

Tango Daly didn't answer, and the call went to voicemail.

Johnny Renza didn't know anything about it at all, and wouldn't until much later, because his super-size skyscraper girlfriend had turned off the police radio overnight.

Homicide Detective Frank Longoria did hear it, and he smiled in his sleep with one word on his lips, whispering it slow and sweet: "Santini".

Two patrol cars arrived at the scene simultaneously, blue lights flashing, none of the officers particularly interested in spending the rest of their shifts as the only living things in this house of the dead. They were training spotlights on the gate when Pop got there.

For some reason, undercover cops love to drive dark-colored, big Ford products. Pop arrived quietly in his version, an ancient navy Fairlane, and out of habit lined it up neatly out of the way, alongside the cemetery fence. You could hardly see it in the dark. He got out and strolled toward the others.

Then more patrol cars with lights and sirens, and a lot of shouting.

"What're you waiting for!"

'Wait hell, what're we *looking* for? What took *you* so long!'"

Then Longoria slid in, in a showy shower of gravel, and in all the excitement he was a little late hitting the brakes on his midnight blue unmarked Crown Vic, and plowed it directly into Pop's car. The Crown Vic's siren let out a pitiful whup-whup through a cloud of radiator steam. When the right rear hubcap on Pop's car finally stopped dancing around the parking lot, there was absolute silence.

CHAPTER TWELVE

B ack at Daly's office, dawn was breaking as he brewed us more coffee. We'd barely gotten out before the cops arrived, and had in fact passed them on the road and kept on going. We figured when they wanted to find us, they would.

I'd kicked off my shoes. Daisy and Daly's .45 were keeping company on his desk.

Pop called to say that Frank Longoria's personal cell phone number had turned up in Wristshot Neely's jacket pocket when they hauled his body out of the hole. Nobody knew exactly what that meant, but it wasn't going to look very good on Frank's resume', and the mob might have something to say about their detective keeping Neely's multi-million dollar diamond secret for himself.

And Willy Short would come out of it okay... better than okay. When things got quiet, he'd climbed out of the hole and, guess what, being the last one standing, he became the unlikely official finder of the six million dollar Grey Goose diamond! Looked like he'd be getting the whole $200,000 reward and he could, god help us, be producing the next big thing in the world of brewing, *Graveyard Digger's Dream*. I only hoped he'd invest first in a 12-Step program. For him, maybe 24 Steps.

Meanwhile, because Daly and I had fired shots, we had reports to write for our records. Better to get it over with now, than piece it together later. An incidental note: it looked like Pop would be driving a new car, compliments of either Frank Longoria or the Buffalo Police Department, whoever wanted to keep that fine detective's depth perception problems quieter.

I leaned back against Daly's desk next to his chair and lingered there, hoping he'd pick up on that. I needed to be close to him. He changed his mind about taking another drink of coffee, and put the mug down. Almost down. In that moment when it hovered above the coaster, he looked up at me and I felt it all the way down to my ankles. He had taken control of the moment.

Purposefully, he rose to face me. His hands took hold of my hip bones, or where my hipbones would be if breakfasts weren't made of butter croissants and coffee with whipping cream in it.

"You sure were at a disadvantage, stuck in that hole," he murmured. "Good thing Delia took a round in her shooting arm when she went down. It also pierced a lung and she lost a lot of blood, but it looks like she'll be around for trial."

"I guess my hours at the range paid off." I gave myself a little pat on the shoulder, and shot him a knowing wink. Sure was exhilarating beating the odds. "In the right hands, a good Sig .380 like Daisy really does the trick."

"Yep, in the right hands, no doubt about it." He worked his way up my rib cage. "Otherwise Delia would have come back for you." He was concentrating on my lips, and it was giving me hot flashes.

"Yep, but she didn't. She was stopped with a single round."

"Yep, a single round," Daly said low, as he pressed his heat against me till I thought I was going to pass out.

His lips brushed mine and never left as he moved in and whispered into my hungry mouth, "Ballistics says it was a .45 ."

"But..."

THE END

... till next time
Turn the page to catch up on the first few pages
of the preceding book,

HELL ON HEELS

the first book of Lynne Russell's
PJ Santini series!

ONE of HELL ON HEELS

"Didn't you forget something?" This private detective boss misses nothing. "They *will* ticket you, if you don't feed the meter."

"No problem," I said. "As of a few minutes ago, I'm also a member of the media. Don't you see the big PRESS sign on the dashboard?"

"Don't you see the blue-and-white up the street?"

"Five bucks says he passes."

"You don't have five bucks."

"Do so." I slapped four ones on his desk, and the three quarters, two dimes and a nickel that would have been parking money.

"I hate to do this Janice, I really do, but you've got to learn," he said as he lifted his toned, tan body out of the chair and pulled a wallet loaded with fifties from his back pants pocket. "Can you make change?" He caught my wrist just as I reached for the big Swarovski crystal paperweight. He'd stepped up his workouts, you could tell right through the silk.

"Your name sure isn't Patience, is it Janice?"

"It isn't Janice, either," as I went for the letter opener. He vice-gripped *that* wrist, and it felt like a million bucks.

"Now what are you going to do?" His eyes were bright with confidence. I was gulping air, inhaling his vitality, taking in the expensive, soft black short-sleeve shirt just slightly darker than his close-cropped hair. He had sea-green eyes and a twelve-month healthy glow.

My gaze just naturally traveled down his pants, because any smart woman would want to maximize the dollars she'd put into her self-defense training; but we were on opposite sides of the desk. "I know," he said leaning over to croon in my ear, "but you wouldn't really do it. You like it like this. I make you hot."

It was a terrible curse. My breathing was labored from close proximity to him and everything he represented – control, excite-

excitement, experience, knowledge, mystery, drop-dead sexiness. To save myself, I exercised my only option: I sank my teeth into his ear.

"Ow! Damn, girl, if you missed a meal just say so!" With his hand clamped up to the side of his head, I couldn't tell whether I'd drawn blood or not. Suddenly he looked like a little boy and I wished I had defended my honor without hurting him. I went around to check.

"You all right? I didn't mean to..."

He took a fast step toward me – the martial artist in him ever alert – and we were nose to nose, breathing the same air again. His high heel-eating plushy carpet wouldn't turn me loose, and I didn't care. This was not the first time we'd played this game, yet I never got any better at it. I wasn't convinced I really wanted to, and still hadn't worked out whether or not he would eventually let me win. All I knew was that he was Tango Daly, the heart and soul of my new adopted home, Iroquois Investigations; the man bad guys hated, women loved and I absolutely...I didn't let myself think about that.

I'm PJ Santini, also known as Janice because my real name is too embarrassing. I'm pretty sure I'm the private eye with the most pairs of four-inch heels in the Tri State Area. I'm also a frequently out-of-work television journalist, mother of a car and a condo I can't afford, daughter of a wacked-out Sicilian earth mother and a retired police sergeant who isn't really retired, and a widow after only two days of marriage. That's right, two days.

"Marry him," Ma had said. "Men are like linoleum. Lay him right the first time... f you can even remember the first time..."

"Ma!"

"...and you can walk all over him the rest of your life." Or for two days.

More importantly, I admit to being slave to the overall lure of dangerous men and dark chocolate. Also by now I'm probably schizophrenic, since this is beginning to make perfect sense. Unfortunately all that sense isn't sitting inside a killer body. At 5'9", I'm too tall to be short and too short to be tall. I'd say my distinguishing feature is the completely off-the-hook curly red hair that rests on my shoulders, except in summer when it frizzes up a good two inches. You can see why I'm grateful for any positive attention.

So far, it had been a day of abnormally positive attention, and this was beginning to scare me. It all began right after I got up when, in desperate need of more income, I'd swallowed my pride along with three cups of coffee, double-double, and a hefty shot of Jack Daniels. I put on matching underwear and ran a blouse through the touch-up cycle in the dryer. Ten ambitious hair rollers burned off dust as they fired up in the bathroom. I moussed and sprayed my hair into submission, and an hour later was in office of the news director at the television station I'd worked at three years earlier. Murray Soper was his name, and I was primed to grovel for a spot on his chain gang. Little did I know that his infamous investigative reporter Gerald Sigmund had mysteriously disappeared, and Soper was one inmate short. All I had to do was ask.

"I just gave the dipshit a month's advance, and now he's gone," Soper whined, eyeing me through the little finger teepee executives make when they want to look brilliant. He was doing what they all do, sizing up the peon trapped in his office, calculating how little he could get me for. I felt more insignificant by the second, sinking deeper into the ratty sofa opposite his big shiny desk. His office was set up like this on purpose, because he had a thing about being short. Not just Boy's Department short, but booster seat short. His mom had squeezed out a store sample, and Murray never stopped taking it personally. The couch was his revenge. So was the desk, which was propped up on four inches of beer coasters. The chair behind it was jacked up so high his toes barely tickled the carpet.

The spasm I was getting in my neck from looking up at him was intimidating, but I decided I'd make up for it later. Right now I really needed money, and the truth was he could get me for a lot less than he thought. I watched in the long silence, as his teeth worked through the dry skin on his lip. When they drew blood, I had to say something.

"Any idea where he went?" I asked, reaching around to tug at my thong. I get nervous around people who can't handle stress. I have found that where there's stress there's shooting, and a lot of the time it's at me.

"I'm clueless," he said, and I totally believed him. "*Find him, damn it Santini, find him!*"

Alright, already. Watching this performance I was mystified, as usual, over what makes males tick. All my life, I've been too willing to give them what they wanted. Take Johnny Renza. It's my personal opinion he's the reason I sucked my thumb into fourth grade. Our families were close from day one, meaning our mothers changed our diapers side-by-side, over and over. This was a recipe for disaster. At such an impressionable age, a girl looks often enough at a hunk like him under those circumstances, and something's gonna palm slapped the desk in rhythm with Ger-ald Sig-mund.

"Tsh. You must be joking. You hire *me* to find another reporter? That's impossible! What am I, psychic? Where would I look for a guy like Siggy?" Then I added, to sound knowingly nonchalant, "He don't run with the traffic." I was sure this would stop him in his tracks. It didn't.

"You're the private eye, break it down," he insisted. "Job's going fast, take it or leave it." This was not working out as I had planned. I just wanted a job...not, you know, *A Job*. I picked at my nails. It'd be nice to afford a manicure again. And I could, by sandwiching a few TV news reports in between Daly's investigative skip traces, and picking up a regular paycheck.

He took aim at the floor and jumped from his chair, stomping imaginary bugs. "What kind of investigative reporter leaves you high and dry?" Rumpelstiltskin wanted to know. "This isn't the first time he's been a horse's arse. Santini, you can produce your own reports on this, at your own pace. Just be available so we can use you for breaking news, too. Siggy's paycheck will be yours. Clear?"

I blinked. Arse? I was going to work for a man who said *arse*?

Made in the USA
Columbia, SC
26 May 2019